Contents

The Gentry: Rebirth

By:
Debbie Nuessle

Far away yet near they be
Always seek on bended knee
In moss and mist, right down the lane
Inside the rose, just after rain
Eye them once, great luck be yours
Seek them ever, your faith be pure...

Reviews

Set in a quaint, historic town in Missouri, The Gentry: Rebirth is an enchanted tale that weaves mystery and fantasy leaving readers captivated.
— K. Stepp

The Gentry evokes feelings of stepping from the familiar into an ethereal world of magic and enchantment and back again. It is an enjoyable mix of fancy and mystery!
— L. Richardson

A magical and mysterious storyline that intrigued me from the beginning. One of those stories you want to read in one sitting. — R. Wolfslau

A tale of whimsy and adventure that will whisk you away. — K. Powers

Dedication

This book is dedicated to all the dreamers who have created their own studio that never sleeps; whether it is a room space or that deeply hidden back corner of the mind. Dream… always dream. For dreams are the true magic in life. They are invisible versions of what is yet to be. Dream hard enough and something longed for appears. Dream hard enough and when the wand is lowered and the pixie dust rests upon the floor, you will proudly face the beautiful reality you have created.

Introduction

The town of Ste. Germaine was rich in history. It was known for its polite people and beautiful gardens scattered among the small yards. More notably, a greatly respected southern French woman lived there. Everyone, even visitors, called her Grandmom. Never had the town been able to tout a lady of such glamour and mystery. She was sought for advice. For her wisdom was thought to descend from greatness and magic. The unexplainable events that occurred at her bed and breakfast, The Petit Jardin, were expected by the towns-people. There was not a September that came and went without some-one catching a glimpse of sparkle. A gossamer veil of mystic came over the skeptical. Those hard at heart only experienced small forms of bad luck; nothing more. Just desserts were served in appropriate measure. As for me, my first September experience was a great many years ago. Then my soul was silenced. Or so they thought. I thank my dear friend, Malvina, for giving me a voice. My soul lives on.
A.B.

Part One

SEPTEMBER 12

It was approaching dusk, that cool September day. The hedgerow framed two sides of the garden. Dark moss circled the oldest tree, a Pine. The other two trees, a Hawthorn and an Elder moved their branches, as if to impress their mentor, the Austrian Pine.

"Come dance with me," came from a voice below.

"But I've never danced. I'll look foolish."

"We might all appear foolish to someone with a mean spirit. Just look at us, all so different. But music and dancing are pure, without judgment. See even the trees seem to enjoy dancing on a night like this. We can make this our best festival yet!"

It was approaching midnight. Their window of time would soon close.

Dance they did. Until they were nearly captured in the light.

Disrepair
With my mind generous in truth...
Pen to paper,
Heart to hand
Telling you this story,
In words you'll understand.

Why come to Ste. Germaine after so many years? To run away, to reconnect with the only family she had left, or to create a new life? The answer wasn't that easy.

Street lamps lit the way as Aubrey entered the quaint and historic town, she was comforted to find so many landmarks, restaurants, and shops from her childhood. There it was. The 'Garden of the Month' sign in Mrs. Parker's yard. When most lawns were losing their luster, hers was still a vibrant green. When most flowers had turned to seed, her garden remained bright and colorful.

There was Annabelle's, the best pies in town. Aubrey brightened up for a moment. Then she recalled why she was here, and how alone she felt. With her mother and father dead and her grandmother living in New York, she would see no familiar faces in this old town. A great deal can change in thirteen years, she thought. Still, she was hoping that the inn would have remained in tact. It was considered historic when she was young. Could its wooden plank floors, thick paned windows, and colorful brocade furniture have stood the test of time?

A twisted version of the past announced itself as she turned down Main Street. The two-story inn had transformed from cheerful to nearly run down. What had happened to the one time marquis place to stay in town? The bed and breakfast with flair and bright character stood no more. The reservations in her purse reminded her that she had no choice. The Petit Jardin Bed & Breakfast would hopefully provide much needed refuge.

No one greeted Aubrey as she pulled onto the once paved side lot. She reflected for a moment that her 2015 Volkswagen was probably her most important and valuable possession. She wrestled with her luggage, and noticed straight ahead, in the back of the yard, there stood a new building, a greenhouse. Its windows were misted over with condensation and there was a door with a number padlock. She wondered if, perhaps, this was the owner's attempt at renovation, at least to the grounds themselves. A greenhouse would mean fresh flowers and greenery.

Much like everything else, the front porch was in need of great repair. The wooden planks creaked beneath her feet as she reached for the door. "Grandmom would not be happy to see all of this wear," she said out loud. Her grandmother owned The

Petit Jardin for a good many years. Aubrey, in fact, was born in the Flora Room just at the top of the stairs, to the right. She double-checked her reservation sheet to see that she would be staying in that very room for the next week, perhaps longer. One hundred dollars a night was a pretty penny, but worth it... she hoped.

She opened the door, smaller than she remembered, yet just as heavy. "I'm sorry I couldn't help with the luggage," came a voice from what she remembered to be the kitchen.

"No worries," she echoed back. "I'm here to stay in the Flora Room. I hope it's still available."

A bent and frail figure appeared at the end of the hall. He was a black man. His hair was grey and his eyes were wise. She followed him into the front room to check in. There it was... just as her grandmother had left it. The thick registry book was opened to the last remaining pages. Aubrey's mind went back to her tenth year when she was allowed to stand at the door and greet guests upon their arrival. That was her last year in Ste. Germaine.

"My name is Merle Travers. You can call me Merle. What's the nature of your stay in this so-called garden town? You're not one of those fancy magazine reporters, are you? Why, they come through all the time. Trampling through people's lawns."

"No, I'm just here for a nice get-away. I used to live in Ste. Germaine when I was younger." Aubrey was reluctant to give too much of her past or present self to this stranger.

"Well, that's enough to get you the Flora Room anyway. What can I call you if I need to?"

As she handed him cash for the week, she answered, "My name's Bree. Can we work out the tax when I check out?"

Merle nodded and turned the book toward her. She felt uneasy as she signed the register. Perhaps later she could sneak a peak at some pages from the past.

"You're still on your own with that heavy luggage, Bree. Hope you can manage. Here's the key. Simple breakfast at 9. Everything's within walking distance. But you already knew that."

"I noticed a metal bistro set in the courtyard. Do you mind if I read a bit out there before walking about town in the morning?"

"Go right ahead. The property is pretty much open. Some folks get a kick out of the big pine with all the rings on its trunk. Over a hundred years old, I guess. Yep, a few chairs for reading there, if you like. There's an old bench, next to the Hawthorn, but it isn't much."

"Thanks Merle."

Aubrey headed up to her room finally feeling like this might have been a good idea. The troubles from her city life were in the rear view for now. She looked forward to a good night's sleep.

The floorboards squeaked at the bottom of the steps. She turned to find Mr. Travers holding himself up with the banister.

"Forgot to mention. The greenhouse is off limits. Not ready for visitors quite yet."

Aubrey caught a glimpse of herself in the dingy full-length mirror on the wall outside her bathroom. She was an average height of five foot five, had long blonde hair, green eyes, and a slender build. She attributed her thinness to two things. First-working outdoors in all types of weather and second-her failed relationship. Her job required a great deal of strenuous exercise. While the other brought stress triggering a loss of appetite. Her move to Ste. Germaine was to bring about a healthier life. A new life.

The Petit Jardin as it used to be...
Tear it down
Then look inside
The magic there
No man can hide.

Aubrey knew a great deal about the bed and breakfast. Her grandmother loved sharing the history of the inn and stories about the guests. Some of her memories seemed more like tales and a bit hard to believe. Those were the most interesting. She also found it curious that she was born there. She often wondered why she wasn't born at the nearby hospital, in Cape Girardeau.

Grandmom, as she was called, owned the inn from July of 1967 until August of 2004. It was a grand place to stay, for its time. Living just across the street she could visit any time she wished. She remembered playing house with her grandmother after school and all summer long. Her mother would allow it only after homework and chores, and
thought it foolish that Grandmom had such an attachment to the business. But Aubrey loved pretending to work there. And Grandmom had her do serious and meaningful tasks, working mostly inside. Grandmom said that the garden took care of itself.

Travelers came from as far away as Europe. Even the townsfolk loved the experience of afternoon tea. Aubrey doubted that Merle Travers carried on that tradition.
There were four magnificently decorated bedrooms; two with private bathrooms. The en suite accommodations were unheard of back in the 1960s. But Grandmom had come into a great deal of money from her gold investments, and wanted to prosper in her family's hometown. Grandmom went from nothing to something overnight. The money allowed her to pay for proper plumbing and an exquisite decor. There was a fifth bedroom, more of a suite really, in the large walk-up attic space. That was Grandmom's room. Aubrey was not allowed up there, ever. She remembered there being fresh flowers in every room of the inn.

At one time, the courtyard was filled with hedges, plants, even a wishing well. Aubrey's favorite area was the bench below the Hawthorn tree. Grandmom called it the thinking bench. Aubrey was never in any trouble to speak of, but she did ask a lot of questions. Grandmom would send her out to the thinking bench to come up with her own answers. Asking about her birth bought her time on the bench. For an hour she traced the embossed scroll designs and watched the motions of the garden. Still, she gained no knowledge, but in the silence of the day she could hear the garden in all of its wonder. Nature was at work. It was almost magical.

There was another tree. Larger than the Hawthorn. It was an interesting Austrian Pine planted in the middle of the garden in 1873 just after the inn was built. Over the years, unusual rings bulged out from the tree almost creating a climbing possibility. Grandmom named the tree Mr. Traurig Schutz. It meant Sad Protector in German. Grandmom thought the tree was sad from being transplanted from its native home of Austria. Of course the tree had grown in the last 13 years. More rings had formed, and the ground below was now absent of flowers and grass. The bench could still be found at the base of the Hawthorn, but greatly needed painting and shimming up.

The wishing well was gone, and Aubrey planned to ask Merle about it. Perhaps he had stored it in the back house or shed. It was quite small, just large enough for a pail or two of water. Young couples staying at the inn threw their pennies in and wished for a glorious future together.

Added to the barren garden was a large and rusty set of wind chimes hanging from the Elder tree. Their sound was deeper than one might imagine for a flower garden. However, with very little to entertain one's sight, the chimes brought an appropriate melancholy tone to the landscape.

Grandmom, Nola Bhaltair
The secrets buried within the age,
Of those who came before
Become tales unleashed to you today,
And give way to so much more.

Aubrey's grandmother was born with the name Nola Bhaltair. She was a very well kept woman, had exquisite posture and a steady attitude. People in the town of Ste. Germaine either respected or hated her. This did not bother Grandmom in the least. She ignored all opinions, even the positive ones. People need to worry about their own gardens, she would say. She did welcome those that sought her opinion, however. Most important to Aubrey was that she and Grandmom shared the same birthday; September 23. They were exactly fifty years apart in age. It was always treated as the most special day of the year, even more so than Christmas. Grandmom called it the Autumn Equinox, and said it was a time for dreaming and making pies. Their birthday would be here in a few weeks. Aubrey hoped if she stayed at the inn long enough Grandmom might come for a visit to make pies and celebrate.

Aubrey's mother, Maire, didn't make much of a fuss over the inn, their birthdays, or anything really. She complained even. Aubrey thought she might be jealous. The great love shown to her by Grandmom made up for the distant relationship she had with her mother. When Maire passed away in her sleep just before Halloween in 2003, Grandmom made Aubrey trick or treat just the same.

Grandmom sat on the thinking bench quite often, and always insisted on being alone. From the Flora Room, Aubrey could see her talking to herself, but never asked about it. Grandmom was wise and imparted her offerings at just the perfect time.

Next to entertaining guests, gardening was Grandmom's most prized way to spend time. She learned the art of grooming nature (as she called it) from an old man who lived in the back house for as long as Aubrey could remember. His name was Pier, short for Pierpone. He ate and slept back there only to come out for Grandmom's gardening lessons. There were never any tools, dirt removal, or what Aubrey would call gardening. Just kneeling and talking. From time to time, Aubrey would catch a glimpse of them separating flower stems, touching a tree, even sitting on the thinking bench. Pier disappeared just before Aubrey's tenth birthday, and was never heard from again. Grandmom did not appear sad, only distant and would not discuss it.

Aubrey followed in her grandmother's footsteps of gardening. With a horticulture degree from St. Louis Community College, she felt quite qualified in saying that the present state of the garden at the inn was ghastly and in need of great grooming. She wondered, with the inn being open, why the outside appearance seemed no longer important?

If her stay was extended, Aubrey planned on asking Merle if she could tend to the garden area a bit, perhaps in exchange for rent. She was excited at the prospect of surprising Grandmom with designs for a beautiful garden if she could talk her into a visit. Celebrating their birthdays together would be the perfect way to make her feel like Ste. Germaine was her home again.

Aubrey did not know much of her grandmother's present way of life. She did know, however, that Grandmom lived in New York. It was believed that thirteen years prior she sold The Petit Jardin in Ste. Germaine, Missouri for six hundred thousand dollars. The property was worth so much more to her grandmother. But it was time to move away in hopes that her granddaughter would have a new, more normal life. Gold that had been stashed away beneath the floorboards in the north parlor was pulled up and tucked neatly into two hatboxes. Grandmom was very traditional and thought hatboxes remained a sign of a lady, still in 2004. It was however to her benefit, when asked if she needed help on her travel to New York. She kindly responded, "Yes, but I can manage my hats, thank you." A New York bank discreetly made the transaction. Grandmom was the only one who knew that there was more gold hidden away in various places throughout the inn. She would, one day, tell Aubrey how she was able to acquire such a fortune.

The past thirteen years brought to her good friends and a relaxed way of living. Being from a small town she did not require elegant amenities. Once she found the perfect mid-rent flat, she furnished it in a style to match her once beloved inn. Fresh flowers, always fresh flowers. That was just enough. Friends would ask, "Why, dear Nola, do you live in such a tiny spot? You surely could live in Manhattan nearer to the entertaining life."

Nola would respond time and again, "My money is meant for growing and New York is not the last stop on my map. A girl with hats, such as myself, needs to keep moving."

SEPTEMBER 13

Girl About Town
Faces you can not recall
Are really not your friends at all
They see in you your wicked past
Hoping that your stay won't last.

Before heading outside, Aubrey grabbed a banana muffin from the kitchen table. Not feeling ready to face the garden in its disrepair, she set out down Main Street. Only one meal a day would be served at the inn, so she would have to do a bit of shopping for things to keep on hand. She made her way to Annabelle's located on Market Street with the intention of buying a sandwich for later.

Circa 1969 the swinging sign read. Annabelle's was a favorite dining spot, known for its sandwiches and pies. Forty-eight years was well past the life expectancy of a small town endeavor. When Aubrey was younger, she often ran to Annabelle's to pick up a pie or two for Grandmom's guests. This was the first time she would dine there. 'Seat Yourself' the sign read. She went to the counter. There it was, by the register, as if time had stood still...the glass case with pies. It held four different flavors, one on each shelf. A roly-poly waitress in a flamingo pink apron, with tattered white lace approached with a menu. The apron certainly clashed with the red and white checked tablecloths.

Then... all of a sudden it seemed as if a small circus was running through the diner.

"Butch, get out here! You won't believe who's come home after all these years! It's little Aubrey from the big fancy inn down the street. How you been girl, what brings you here...

how's that grandma of yours? Still livin' up in fancy town? Grandmom didn't die, did she? Butch you gotta see this!"

People were leaning and looking. Even folks on the sidewalk could hear the commotion, and stopped to window shop for gossip. Butch finally came out, obviously irritated that his grillwork had been interrupted. Not ashamed of his ways, he blurted out, "Did you leave all them magical tricks where you came from? Or did you come to dig some old ones up in that run down garden?"

"Why that's no way to welcome back one of our own. You might not remember us, but I'm Doris and this here's Butch. You used to come and buy pies and things for the inn. You mostly picked up the blackberry. Your grandma trusted you with important tasks back then. Such a sweet little girl you were. Butch you just keep quiet. The past is in the past. Them were just witches tales anyways."

Doris was genuine and confident in trying to put Aubrey at ease, but Butch seemed very convinced of something. Aubrey made her way to the door with her turkey sandwich wrapped up to go. Distracted, she headed further down Market Street. Her mind was filled with unknowns. If only she could talk with Grandmom. As she made her way through the short blocks of Ste. Germaine, what was once familiar on her drive in, seemed to hold the same mystery as Annabelle's. When she reached Third Street, a little boy riding a red bike stopped right on the sidewalk in front of her.

He looked her straight in the eyes and said, "You must be the witch everyone is talking about. If you ever need me to dig up those bones in the garden, just let me know!" He peddled off in the opposite direction.

Halloween, she thought, is just around the corner. But why so much talk about witches, magic, and bones? Aubrey couldn't wait to get back to her dusty room to relax and empty her mind.

Merle called to Aubrey as she opened the door to the inn. "I have more muffins fresh from the oven for tomorrow's breakfast. Blueberry this time. You are welcome to take one up to your room if you like. Also, you may have noticed we have a couple that just arrived. I placed them in the Hedgerow room here on the first floor. Better privacy for everyone. Did you enjoy your trip through garden town?"

"You know, Merle, I didn't even notice the gardens. Maybe tomorrow. If you're sure about the muffin, I may eat it later. Does the little fridge in my room work? I brought a sandwich back."

"It sure does."

Up in the Flora Room, Aubrey used a small hand towel to dust here and there throughout. She didn't want to hurt Merle's feelings, but was quite sure he didn't have a staff to help him out. By the way he leaned on things, he probably didn't get upstairs too often. This was nothing like Grandmom's way of running things. She had Pier the gardener, a cook who enjoyed making anything and everything but pies, and a maid. Aubrey couldn't recall to whom Grandmom sold the inn, but she was sure it wasn't Mr. Travers. Yet another question on her list.

She finally admitted it might be time to unpack. Her stay in 'garden town' was real, though the uneasiness of life that brought her here seemed to be traded for something lurking in the shadows in ways she couldn't describe. As she found the drawers still lined with lilac parchment paper, she wondered what the guests downstairs might be thinking. Was their room dusty? Had they stayed here before? Will she be able to chat with them in the garden? Aubrey ate half of the blueberry muffin then placed it into the fridge with her sandwich. She slept well that night with the solemn notes from the wind chimes floating over the sill of her half-opened window.

Some people see
Some people hear
Some never do
But magical folk are always near
At times, right next to you.

SEPTEMBER 14

The next morning, the song of the wind chimes was mixed with a slight silvery chill. Before shutting the window, Aubrey spotted that same boy on the red bike riding up and down the sidewalk in front of the inn. He had dark brown hair and a huge grin upon his face. His clothes were simple, yet in style…a pair of jeans and a Nirvana t-shirt.

Aubrey shouted, "Good morning!"

"Good morning," the little boy shouted back. "My name's Telford. Telford Chasseur. My great-granddad built this fence." With that, he road off quickly down the walk. What an interesting young man, she thought.

"Merle, will the couple be joining me this morning?"

"No, I'm afraid not. I heard a bit of squabbling earlier. The young man left out the front door in a hurry, and his fiancée left by way of the back door. She might be in the garden if you'd like to take her a plate."

"Yes, of course. Merle, leave the dishes and I will do them a bit later."

"Oh, I couldn't ask that of you. You're the guest."

"That may be Merle, but I'd love you to save your energy for more important things… like the garden perhaps."

"Do you have the green thumb like your grandmother?"

Surprised, Aubrey responded, "Did you know Grand-mom?"

"Let's save that for after dishes. It's worth a good sit-down. Not the kind of talk you hurry with a plate in one hand. Now go tend to that wide-eyed young lady in the garden. You're not that old yourself, but something tells me wisdom's been planted inside your soul. Now go on."

"Good morning. I brought you a plate," Aubrey announced to the girl sitting in one of the metal chairs. Her legs were pulled up to her chest as if to keep warm.

"I'm Aubrey. Merle suggested I bring you a plate. Come, sit with me by the tree."

"Are you sure?" she responded.

"Absolutely. This tree is very special, and my grandmother used to call this the thinking bench. When I was little she sent me out here a few times a week to figure things out for myself."

"Thank you for the plate, but I don't feel like eating," she said as she wiped her face.

"I've had one of Merle's muffins. They're good and a bit dry at the same time. But how can you go wrong with a few strips of bacon?"

She took the plate and said, "I'm Patty... here with my fiancé Jack. We're kind of in an argument right now over my mother's involvement in the wedding. This getaway was supposed to be our time to relax before the big day. But the same issues keep popping up."

Aubrey noticed the bruising on Patty's arm, and the darkness on her left eye under her sunglasses. "Honestly, Patty. There are times when a woman needs more than a thinking bench and an old Hawthorn tree to field the important questions in life. Can your mother help? Do you have a best friend?"

"I suppose. They're both in Cape Girardeau right now. I should just figure this out."

A man appeared at the fence. "Who's this?" he said pointing at Aubrey.

Patty responded, "This is Aubrey."

He grabbed Patty's arm. "What did you tell her?"

Quickly, Aubrey left the couple to handle things. The relationship she had left behind in St. Louis was nothing like this. But her experience told her that it would be far better to end things now, than end up in a violent marriage. She was sorry, but knew it wasn't her place to offer advice.

"Merle, I've finished the dishes, and I'm ready for our talk. Are you about to surprise me?"

"Well the truth is... there are lots of versions of the truth. And surprises are infinite. Now what that means for you is good fortune in very small doses. For instance...the money you gave me for your room went straight into a bank account."

"Well of course, I'd expect you to put the money in the bank."

"It's sitting in an account with your name on it. Your grandmother gave me very clear instructions. And when it comes to dealing with Nola Bhaltair I've always played along and played fair." Merle went on, "Now by the look on your face you have no idea what's taking place. So let me do the talking for a while. And don't forget to take a few deep breaths. I find it helps in times of great confusion."

Aubrey sat down in the kitchen chair closest to the wood-burning stove. There was a comforting warmth. With hands folded on her lap, she readied herself for the unknown.

"Miss Nola Bhaltair is a woman of great power and great mystery. In her defense, she does not use her power unless absolutely pushed. Her mysterious side, on the other hand, is something that is constant to those who know her best. Why, I'm certain that those high society folks in Tinsel Town have no idea who she really is. No, they do not know her as I do."

"Merle, I think I know my Grandmom better than anyone."

"You do, now, do you? Why did she move to New York only to live in a tiny rat's house? Do you know where your grandmother is right now, really?"

"Merle, you have been very nice to me. Yet, now I find your actions peculiar, and quite frankly, scary."

"Aubrey, you are the reason your grandmother does everything. She wants the world to be better for you. And she wants you to get to know the world you really belong to. Soon she'll be here to explain more of this to you. Until then, you live here for free, and I am more than obliged to accept your talents on grooming the garden. And no more pretending your name is Bree."

Convinced that Merle Travers was more than he appeared, Aubrey went over to him with tears in her eyes. "Is Grandmom safe?"

"Your grandmother remains forever safe, and you, my child, are about to embark on countless journeys. This inn and the town of Ste. Germaine are very fortunate that you have returned. There is a reason you felt compelled to come back home. And rest assured, your life is heading in a new direction."

SEPTEMBER 16

The arguing from the Hedgerow suite continued, creating a cloud of sadness at the inn.

"What can we do for them, Merle?" Aubrey asked.

"This is not a matter for you to worry about. Solutions come when you least expect them. If things don't work themselves out, then Miss Bhaltair will handle things. The Petit Jardin has its ways. The garden has its way."

"Now that I know you're somewhat acquainted with Grandmom, you're riddles come in more frequent batches. Patty and Jack are surely a couple destined down a dead end road. I ran back to 'garden town' because I thought it was my only answer. My own life was a dead end road. I'm here, now. Merle, you know what's next for me, don't you?"

It was the first time she had seen Merle smile. It wasn't the type of smile that makes you smile back. In fact, he appeared all knowing and quite sure of himself.

"Pardon my reaction to 'somewhat'. Your grandmother has given me certain instructions. Giving you all of the answers was not included. She will be here in a matter of days, if not sooner. What happens between now and then remains to be seen. In the meantime, you are welcome to have a visit to the thinking bench."

Aubrey was not one to wait for Grandmom to help solve life's puzzles. Heading to the registry book in the south parlor, she was determined to find answers. Her mission was dashed as she heard a strange voice from behind the curtains of the parlor.

"Do not be alarmed," said a small brown figure. He wasn't a black man like Merle. His skin appeared to be burnt from the sun, perhaps.

Aubrey sat down on a settee near the table. Breathe, she thought. Merle said I should breathe. He spoke up in a voice like that of a tiny, yet confident, mouse. "Allow me to introduce myself. And might I add that you did not invite me. I am more accustomed to an invitation by way of cheese, wine, a few crumbs perhaps. On this occasion, I, in fact, have invited myself to be a part of your utterly confused situation. I blame most, if not all of this, on you. Merle told me to use my restraints. You, my dear, call for special measures. You are pleasant enough, to be sure. However, your spirit could use a bit more sparkle. You are in need of a reason to be brave. The doomed couple in the Hedgerow Room require a stern touch, but it won't be at your hand. Did I catch sight of you praying for them last evening? A kind act, to be sure."

"I was praying for them. How did you know, who are you, what are you?" Breathe... Aubrey tried desperately to stay calm. Her whole life here at the inn was becoming more confusing by the minute.

Before her, stood the strangest little man. Large feet with separated toes held up a diminutive creature covered in fur. He stood about two feet tall, had mouse-like ears, and wore a small sieve on his head.

"My name is Ignatius Porteur. I am a brownie. Please do not mistake me for an elf, a fairy, and most of all a gnome. My reason to be is most unlike the list so mentioned. My reason to be is my most favorite thing of all things. The fire of the house is my place to collect, and I am the gatekeeper of the entrance. My stature is small, but my tasks are without bounds. I must leave you now. Time moves quickly as we speak and the time grows near as we are idle. Nola Bhaltair is almost here."

With a steadfast, yet lumbered gait, Ignatius Porteur was gone. My wits are fading, Aubrey thought. Was she going crazy or do people, in truth, have nightmares so real that blurred lines make living surreal? Aubrey forgot all about the guest registry, and could think only of going upstairs to rest. Where is Grandmom?

SEPTEMBER 17

I'll reveal these secrets now
Use them as you will
Some are meant to save
Some are meant to kill.

"What have we discussed and agreed upon? Solutions should be clean and fast. Not a trace left behind. Why is this insignificant Jack still beating his fiancée about the face, neck, and limbs? A rock has more respect for a hiker that pounds its boots upon the trail."

"Grandmom, you've arrived! Why are you talking about Patty and Jack? Do you know them from New York?"

"Aubrey, please listen closely. Wisdom can be found in worlds you've never considered. You do not need answers to everything this very moment. I don't mean to be harsh, but I've just arrived. Already... so many questions."

Thoughts raced through Aubrey's head. Wasn't this supposed to be a joyous reunion? And how did Merle know her grandmother?

"Grandmom, I'm older now. This is not the time to send me to the thinking bench."

"Oh, but my dear, it is. Every visit to the bench is productive, and it is better for you to be there than here. I must speak with Merle." All at once Nola Bhaltair pointed toward the garden.

Aubrey had never been sent to the thinking bench like this before. Fighting back tears, with nowhere to go, Aubrey ran from the house and down the street.

" Hey wait up! Hey, you, whay are your running?" It was the boy on the red bike.

"Please go away!" Aubrey stopped running.

"Remember me? I'm Telford." He hopped off his bike and pushed it along as he walked beside Aubrey. "Why are you so upset? Let me guess... you started digging in the garden."

Aubrey stopped suddenly and grabbed Telford by the shoulders. "Now, listen to me. I am through with mixed up words and things that have nothing to do with me... things that have no meaning. Just leave me alone." She smoothed out Telford's shirt and turned away.

"Maybe you didn't ask the right person," he said. Telford hopped on his bike and yelled back to Aubrey, "I'll meet you at Annabelle's. You can buy me a sandwich."

They sat across from each other in the booth by the window. Telford waved at Doris. With a wink, she approached ready to take their order.

Telford spoke up. "I'll have a BLT, but hold the lettuce and the tomato. You know, just like I like it. My new friend will have a slice of apple pie. By the way, Doris, when is your break?"

"Honey, you know I own this place. I'm the boss and can take a break anytime I want. What do you have in mind?"

"We have a question or two that might make...Hey what's your name?" he asked turning to his new friend.

"Aubrey Bhaltair."

"Doris, your version of things might help Aubrey feel better about coming back to Ste. Germaine."

"Let me square away the other customers and I'll be right back."

Doris took orders, cleaned tables, and served. She was a very happy lady in her mid sixties, and bounded brightly about the diner. Butch, on the other hand, was not so cheerful. Aubrey noticed him peering from the cook's window behind the counter. His face was scowled up and ugly. Years of harsh remarks and negativity had probably laid claim to the aging of his face. He did not speak to Aubrey, and she was relieved. Doris squeezed in beside Telford.

"Hey, kid, make some room for me. So what is it you want to know? I can only tell you the things that developed as rumors and hearsay back when Aubrey was little, and before your time youngin'. These tales were mostly entertaining to intelligent people such as myself. Others, though, believed everything they heard and wanted to close the inn down."

The tears were gone now. In the past half hour her sadness had turned to anger.

Aubrey spoke up. "I'd like to start with something simple, something that seems so trivial. Telford, why is it important that your great-granddad built the fence around the inn? And why are you so eager to dig up bones in the garden?"

Doris spoke first, "Those are excellent questions. Telford's knowledge is brand new knowledge. I'll be interested to hear this, as well.

"This is going to be easy! My 4th grade research paper assignment was supposed to be about an interesting family member, and I chose Robert Chasseur. My facts must have been pretty straight because Mrs. Bonet gave me a B plus. Robert Chasseur was my great, great, great granddad. There were really a few more greats, but Mrs. Bonet said that wouldn't be necessary. I think she might have thought I wanted to cheat on my word count. Anyway, he worked for the Iron Mountain Mines way back in 1855. The mine had been around a while before that. Granddad got into the business when a railroad was built between St. Louis and Pilot Knob. His job was a clean job. I mean he didn't have to dig up the iron. He just sold it to people who could make things out of it. He finally went to work for one of his customers. It was a fence company. This, I guess, was before white picket fences were so popular. So he sold fences and gates. It was probably a fib to say he made the fence at the old inn. Sorry about that. He did sell it to someone way before your family came along, though. I didn't know their name, but Mrs. Bonet said that was okay, too."

Doris spoke up, "Telford, aren't you leaving out the most important part?"

"Oh, yep, I sure am. This is the cool part, too. Probably what got me that high grade. Well, my granddad came along at just the right time. You see, the owners were talking about fairies being in the garden, and people around here knew that fairies do not like iron. You know Superman gets all weak around kryptonite. Well, that's the same for fairies and iron. So the owners thought they could keep the fairies out. But... it kept the fairies in, so the story goes. Guess that's what started so many rumors, since the fairies could never go away. But, I always wondered what could a tiny fairy do anyhow? I wish I could show you my research paper. I asked Mrs. Bonet for it back, but she said it was a fine enough example to show her future students. Neat, huh?"

"Hey Doris, the diner's closing in fifteen minutes," yelled Butch from the kitchen.

"No need to hurry me, Butch."

Doris took care of the last few customers and Telford went on to talk about the bones in the garden.

"Are you sure you want to know this part?" Telford asked.

Aubrey no longer thought of her grandmother. The garden is the mystery. The garden has answers. "Yes, of course, the fairy story was harmless enough. However, I'm not sure I believe it."

The sun began to hide away and Telford knew he had to be home soon. "Gotta make this part quick. Tales I've heard say that when a fairy and a not fairy person get married they can have a fairy baby. From what my mom has told me, most non-magical people hate fairies. Well, twin fairies were born. This was before my time, but not too long ago. The tales I've heard say there is a tiny iron cage buried somewhere below the earth in the garden at the inn."

"What is in the iron cage?"

"Oh, I can tell you that," answered Doris, "just one fairy. Or should I say one set of fairy bones?"

Aubrey almost forgot about her encounter with Ignatius, but would not dare to add it to those tales shared in Annabelle's Diner that day. She knew she must be more reasonable with Grandmom and earn the trust of Ignatius the Brownie.

Telford and Aubrey walked out of the diner.

"How far do you live?"

"Oh, not far. Just a few houses down on Third. My mom works late most nights, so she won't be worried."

"Telford, how do you know so much about all of this? I feel foolish that I am just now learning these things about the inn."

"My mom told me and her mom told her." Telford started to pedal off... "Say, Aubrey, you think we can be friends?"

"I could really use one."

"Awesome, and don't forget I'm pretty strong for my size and I got a shovel."

The iron fence was four feet tall and went around the whole property, except for the side parking area. Aubrey let her fingers drag across each spine until she arrived at the gate. She thought to herself, the gate is never closed so why can't fairies come and go? Patty was sitting at the top of the first tier of wooden steps before the landing.

"Thanks for trying to help me before. It's obvious I'm a mess. I suppose it's no secret what kind of man my Jack has shown himself to be."

"That's okay. I've been where you are. Just when you think you've got life all sewn up, you're hit in the belly with a hard jab."

"You seemed so put together when I first met you, but something is bothering you. I can tell."

"Things were fine when I lived in St. Louis. A little college degree I earned landed me a job at The Missouri Botanical Gardens. I loved it there, but my world changed when I met this guy... Daniel. I hoped Ste. Germaine would help me breathe, open my eyes, and most of all give me direction for my future. When Grandmom arrived things became a bit topsy-turvy. Don't get me wrong, I love my grandmother, and I'm glad to be done with men for a while. I just want to relax and garden. That's it."

"I feel the same way, about men that is. Thank goodness Jack and I aren't from the same town."

"What do you mean?"

"He's gone. I told him to leave, and I hope he never ends up here or in Cape Girardeau again. That's my home, not his. And he complained the whole time he was there. I'm such a fool, to think I could change a grouchy man like him. Your grandmother, such a sweet lady, she ordered a rental car for him. And Mr. Travers offered him a slice of freshly baked pie. No hard feelings, I guess. The Petit Jardin really is a great place to stay. In fact, I can see why you love this town. One more day, then I'm back to Cape."

Aubrey spoke up, "It's old to me, and new to me all at once. The next time you come to visit, and I hope you will, the inn will be more grand than it is right now."

"You have some plans for renovation?"

"The inn just needs a little maintenance and updating here and there. It's the garden I would really love to spruce up. A long time ago, when I was a little girl, the garden had flowers everywhere, a lovely walking path, and a sweet wishing well."

"Considering what has gone on in my life these past few days, I would love to throw a penny or two into a wishing well. Is it usually meant only for young love?"

"Not at all. I made a lot of wishes when I was little."

"Any of them come true?"

"I suppose so, but it's bad luck to tell them out loud. Maybe Merle knows where it might be. I'm sure it needs a fresh coat of paint."

"Check out is at two o'clock tomorrow. If he puts it out before I leave I can help you with it. It will help me take my mind off things."

Aubrey left Patty on the front steps. She knew it was time to face her grandmother.

"Aubrey, Aubrey Bhaltair! You seem to be in a different world today. And you are still my granddaughter. No more running off like a child."

"It was in my running off, Grandmom, that I discovered I was not treating you fairly. My patience, respect, and sensibility have surfaced."

"That's more like it. A reasonable assistant is most welcome at the inn. Isn't that right, Merle?"

Merle answered, "Yes, of course."

"Grandmom, I am not an assistant, and I will gladly be the granddaughter of old if you are honest with me. For starters, is Ignatius a reasonable assistant? And is he what he seems to be?"

"I did tell him to make your acquaintance. And, yes, of course. He would not be in my employ…"

A very loud clearing of the throat could be heard from the kitchen.

"In fact, let me clarify. He does not work for me. He simply enjoys keeping track of the house, its occupants, tidiness, and safety. I do not employ him. It is his life's work, a calling if you will. Brownies, much like fairies, do not desire payment or gratitude. A simple sip of wine or a few breadcrumbs will suffice. Do not cross these boundaries, my dear. Unhappy magical folk are, in the very least, unhappy."

"In my patience, dear Grandmom, I'm gathering that what you know has been shared with Merle and Ignatius. What I am yet to know will be given to me in bits and pieces over time. Is this correct?"

"It is, sweet Aubrey. You shall not be expected to undertake any task large or small, whether it be knowledge or action, in too short a time. We here at The Petit Jardin have managed an open-mindedness that spans over a great many years. Do not fret. And keep your new friends close."

"New friends?"

"Why, Merle and Ignatius, of course. Patty is simply a mere acquaintance. And you are doing marvelous in that regard."

"Grandmom, I do love you."

"As I do you. Don't think I've forgotten the celebration of our birth dates. Memorable to be sure."

SEPTEMBER 18

"Merle, thank you so much for the effort of finding and

placing the wishing well. It will be beautiful, just as it was before. Do we have any spare paint on the property?"

"We may, and I will look. Please know that Ignatius was the keeper of the well. He did the hiding and uncovering of it. And of course it is far too heavy for me to lift. He thought this would be the proper place."

"Oh, it is. Just as it was when I was little. I'll walk with you to see about that paint."

Patty came out with her suitcases. "After I put my things in the car, I can help you with the well."

Aubrey walked with Merle. The greenhouse was to the right as they walked down the gravel path toward the shed. "Where did Ignatius find the wishing well?"

"Not for us to know, I guess. Just glad he was nice enough to get it out for you. It's commendable that you hope to change this place... Just remember Nola Bhaltair is the keeper of the inn. No matter how you hope to make things different. She has her visions."

"You make it sound like she owns the inn. All this time, I've assumed you owned it."

"Grandmom never sold it."

"Then how did she help me with college? How did she manage a life in New York City?"

"She has her means."

"Merle, with all the surprising news, you certainly must admit that I've been pretty patient up until now?"

"That may be, but with Nola as our leader, you...we... have no choice."

"Leader?"

"There you are," called Patty, "are we ready to put some new life into this old wishing well?"

"It's amazing that she can be so positive," mumbled Merle.

"Never mind about that," Aubrey whispered back.

"Hey Patty, Merle's just about to show us to the paint and brushes."

"Here we go," said Merle as he opened up the shed.

"We need two colors. One for the top, one for the bottom."

"What about a bucket?" Patty asked. "Isn't there always a bucket that goes up and down."

"Yes, I do remember there being one." Aubrey answered. "It never moved, but a third color would be great. We'll take all the paint and those brushes over there."

Aubrey and Patty toted the supplies back to the wishing well. Merle followed with a large tarp.

"It was great of you to help us, Merle. We'll take it from here."

The two talked most of the afternoon. Painting the wishing well was a good distraction. Just being with someone was an important bonus for them both. When the wishing well was nearly finished, Merle appeared with the inn's phone.

"Miss Patty, there is a call for you."

"Hello... no... how...of course, I'll stay right here." She began to cry.

"What is it?" Aubrey asked.

"The highway patrol... they said they found Jack dead in his car down an embankment. They're taking him to the St. Louis County Coroner's office. I guess he was headed north. How could he have died, how?"

"Oh, Patty, I'm so sorry. Do they need you to meet them there?"

"No. His identification was in order. I was only called because his mother had asked them to. They are having a local officer come here to question me. How horrible. I'm going to have to face his parents, at one point, I suppose."

"I'll stay with you until the policeman arrives. Let's take a break... come on... over here." She motioned toward the bench. "The wishing well is not important. I can start back up tomorrow.

"No, we need to finish the job. I don't want to be remembered for the bickering couple in the Hedgerow Room. Or the girl whose fiancé died after they broke up. Let's get back to it."

Aubrey spoke. "His health seemed in good condition. Did he take care of himself?"

"Yes, but his work was always pretty stressful. Do you think he could have had a heart attack?"

"I'm sure his parents will have answers when you speak with them."

Dear Reader, If you'll allow, I'd love to float on in. Jack did not have a heart attack. Being the selfish man that he was, Jack gladly accepted the pie from Merle Travers, left the room bill for Patty, and set off down the road. What he did not take into consideration, nor did he have any reason to, was the untraceable poisonous berries in that very slice of pie. He was a very mean man. In the underworld of elegance, purity, and fairness he was not welcome. The berries in the pie would not be considered, as they would be unidentifiable in an autopsy report. Patty was questioned only in regards to his health and why he was by himself. Her bruising was not discovered, and she was sincerely surprised and heartbroken. She was not a suspect. Having a police car pull up in front of the iron fence that day in Ste. Germaine only gave folks more to talk about. Grandmom was unflinching and said all the right things. A.B.

Aubrey discovered the bottom was simply an old barrel with wood around it. She and Patty went on to paint it and fashioned it back to its proper beginnings, directly between the Hawthorn and Elder trees. Limited by color choices, they painted the base white, and the roof light blue. Aubrey mentioned that flowers were sure to stand out against the white base. The bucket, which was only for show, was painted brown. It was easy enough to reassemble, having only the three makeshift pieces. They used the hose from the side of the inn to fill it.

Patty and Aubrey took turns throwing a penny into the well, each making a special wish. And as they did the sun cast a shimmery light through the branches of the trees in the garden. This was the first time, since coming back, that Aubrey felt there was life in the garden. Would their wishes come true? There was no way to know what Patty wished for. Nor did she ever return to the inn. Aubrey wished for answers.

It was later that Aubrey would discover the answers as thus: Grandmom did not need a wishing well to create the future. The future was at her hand. Her powers adjusted the future to create a better world. She had the underworld. The powers of the garden were easy, to be sure, and would one day be turned over to Aubrey. The strength of the greenhouse belonged to Merle.

"I have to go now, Aubrey. Thank you so much for making this horrible ordeal manageable."

"We'll meet again, I'm sure. You have my cell, don't you?"

"I do. I'd love for my mom and dad to see this old place. Cape is not that far. Bye Aubrey."

They hugged goodbye as new friends, or special acquaintances do. Aubrey stood at the wishing well and watched Patty drive away down Main Street. Time to plan a birthday celebration. She wondered if Brownies were to be included on the guest list? If not, it would just be Grandmom, Merle, and Telford. She would speak with Ignatius to avoid hurt feelings. There would be a thimble of wine and tidbits of cheese for later, just to be sure.

Grandmom entered the garden without notice. "Did Patty make her start back to Cape?" She asked.

"Yes, she did. She'll be doing a lot of thinking on her trip home. She seems to be close with her parents, and that's a good thing. I haven't been around death much in my life. Except when Mother died. You insisted that death was inevitable and tears could not change fate... That lesson made it easier for me to leave St. Louis and come here for a new start. Knowing I couldn't change things made my decision easier. Can you change what is yet to be, Grandmom?" Aubrey asked.

"In your calmness, I hear patience and a thirst for the truth. The truths that I will share little by little and bit by bit will bring you wisdom. That wisdom will gain you power. Most of all that power is weighted down with responsibility. Are you prepared for all of this, my dear?"

"Does Merle have all of this?" Aubrey wanted to know. Over the past few days she had come to respect the gentle and consistent mystery of his actions.

"Yes, as does Ignatius. There are a few others that you will meet in time. Sit with me, here, on the bench."

Grandmom reached for Aubrey's hand. She went on. "First, we are going to start in the present. No going forward or back. Jack was responsible for his own life. No one else. It does not matter how he died. He decided to be worthless. In this garden, in this house, if worthless cannot be fixed...then out it goes. Both Merle and I spoke with Jack, and he would not listen to reason. He even tried to hurt Merle. A pie was delivered, a car was called for, and that was that. See those lovely hedges over there...the ones near the greenhouse? Those are Privet Hedges. The entire plant is poisonous. The black berries especially. Once ingested they shut down the kidneys, create high blood pressure. These things result in death within two hours. He had discussed his trip home, the route and time, with Merle while eating his pie. Aubrey, here at the inn, all plans are perfect."

"Oh, Grandmom, I can't believe you and Merle killed a man. And now the knowledge is mine. How could you?"

"Remember, sweet Aubrey, he chose to be worthless."

"This raises a new question! I fetched pies from Annabelle's for you when I was little. Why? And what else is poisonous in the garden? How is one to know?"

"These are very smart questions. Using Annabelle's pies adds to the illusion. And the garden is extremely safe. We have eyes on everything and everyone. No one has ever died unless it was meant to be."

"Please don't tell me that there have been others!" Aubrey pleaded.

"Only a few, but deserving. Those are minor details. When you reached your ten years, I could clearly see you would need to know things. A ten year old is not yet ready for the truths of their other life. So I sent you to boarding school, pretended to sell this lovely inn, then went to New York. It was to be a whole new beginning for us. I received word that you were going to come back to Ste. Germaine, so I did the same. Merle did a fine job keeping an eye on you for a few days. Jack was not part of the plan. But so be it. Eventually, all will be revealed."

"How did you know I was coming?"

"It is everywhere that I know special people. They are very helpful to me. Many have watched out for you over these past years."

"Please don't tell me that you killed Daniel."

"Heavens, no! He wasn't worthless, just not meant for you. We don't go around killing for sport, dear."

"Grandmom, may I tell you what I think I know so far?"

"Of course, my dear."

"There's a rather friendly Brownie living in the house. He takes care of the hearth and protects us. Merle is a kind man who uses Annabelle's pies to insert poisonous berries. The pies are then used to do away with worthless people. This is considered suicide not homicide. You know things, many things, and you are going to share them with me. Does that sum it up?"

Grandmom nodded her head while Aubrey spoke, then interjected, "You are catching on. And this is precisely why you are forbidden to keep a diary." Grandmom laughed out loud. "All things that you hold in disbelief may be the things that others will misinterpret. Simply because things are hard to understand does not make them untrue."

"How so?"

"Do you believe in Ignatius?"

"Yes."

"Do you want him harmed?"

"Of course not."

"Then he is what we call a property secret. Ignatius exists only to us. Who is the nastiest man you have met in the past few days? Besides that dreadful Jack, of course."

"Butch, I guess."

"The things he yelled at you, he does not understand. Does that make them untrue?"

"I'm not sure. Does it?"

"Enough for today. All of this truth telling has exhausted me from the inside out. Our birth date celebration is approaching."

"May I plan it?"

"Of course you may, my dear."

SEPTEMBER 19

"It isn't that I'm ashamed of you... it's just that I would like both of you at the celebration, and I'm not sure that Telford needs to know that a Brownie lives behind the hearth at The Petit Jardin. Let's face it, you have pointy ears. In a perfect world I'd sprout fairy wings and fit right in. But that isn't the case. Telford is a nice young man. But if I have to choose, I choose you."

"Nice it is most definitely, but not necessary. My appearance is of no concern. Worry not. There is a remedy for that. I will not disappoint you, and it will all work out to be a fine party. I've seen Telford about, and he does seem likable. A very curious young lad, though, as I had to encourage him away from the greenhouse last week."

"How did you manage that?"

"With a rock to the middle of his back, of course. Fear trumps curiosity every time."

"You are a unique little man Ignatius. Will you be having wine and cheese crumbs at the party?"

"Absolutely not. To serve others is a Brownie's duty. I may not eat in front of you to be sure. Telford will not notice. I will see to that. After the celebration, you are welcome to leave a few morsels near the hearth."

"Ignatius, should I wait to ask about your transformation?"

"Most certainly. Let it be known that Merle does like his wine, and will gladly help the festivities along with his consumption of a glass or two. Music will be shared, of course."

"You have been a great help Ignatius!"

"Let it also be known, Miss Aubrey, Brownies make good friends. Best of all we can not tell lies."

Aubrey found Grandmom in the check-in parlor. "Grandmom, do you have suggestions for the party menu?"

"You are handling the gathering, Aubrey. I have other things to attend to. However, I do request that it be at six o'clock sharp. I understand young Telford will be joining us. That should put him home at a proper hour. I was surprised that you assumed his mother would grant permission."

"Oh, I hadn't thought of that."

"Not to worry. What you don't know is Telford's mother and I have known each other for many years. She is an open-minded woman. Her fairness of spirit has molded Telford into a truth seeker. He is a truth seeker without judgment."

"Grandmom, your riddles are endless."

Part Two

BIRTHDAY, SEPTEMBER 23

Aubrey helped Merle move a table and a few more chairs to the garden. The fall air was perfect that day. "Merle, let's use the thinking bench on one side. That way we won't need as many chairs."

"Good idea. You were busy in the kitchen today. What is on the menu?"

"I tried to think of everyone. There will be cookies for Telford, a cheese and cracker tray, and Annabelle's made up two deli sandwiches that I've cut into portions. There will also be a small cake. I've instructed Ignatius to give a nod at his favorites, so I can leave a bit out later tonight. He's such an interesting fellow."

"Are you speaking about me, Miss Aubrey?" asked Ignatius as he entered through the iron gate.

"Oh, my. How in the world did you manage this?" she asked.

Ignatius grinned. Aubrey could not believe her eyes. Her new friend had somehow grown three feet taller. His face was that of a handsome young man. And his attire was casual and neat.

"Do you approve?"

"I do, Ignatius, but please tell me you can go back to your quaint little self after the party."

"Of course I can. This is a fine fit to be sure, but I do prefer being a traditional Brownie."

"Come help with the food."

Just then Telford arrived carrying a small gift. "I'm here,"

41

he announced with a great big smile.

"Oh, Telford! I thought I said no gifts."

"It's only for you. My mom told me that Grandmom refuses gifts."

"She does, in fact."

Merle and Grandmom came from the house to join the celebration. Merle was carrying a finely embroidered red bag. Lights from the inn and the greenhouse created the perfect glow. Mist hovered from beyond the hedges and the Privet berries gave off a shimmer.

"The wine is delicious, Grandmom."

"So is the grape juice," said Telford. He and Aubrey clinked glasses and giggled.

"Not too much for you, Aubrey. You need your slumber to be unaltered. This marks the beginning of your twenty-third year. This is the first night of a very special year ahead. Let's everyone raise our glasses to the moon and say, 'I honor you'," said Grandmom.

And they did. After the toast Merle took from his bag what appeared to be a very large harmonica. He entertained the guests for a few minutes. The low and mysterious notes were calming to everyone.

"Merle, what is that lovely instrument?" Aubrey asked.

"It is called a pan-flute or a panpipe. A dear friend brought it back from Greece many years ago. He gave it to me just before his death. It can only be mastered by certain beings."

"Hey, Aubrey, open your gift!" Telford said.

Within the clumsily wrapped paper Aubrey found a snow globe with a beautiful fairy inside.

"Mom helped me pick it out. You and I don't have many friends. The fairy inside looks so happy. I thought it might make you smile."

"This is a wonderful gift, Telford. Thank you. My nightstand will make a perfect home. Grandmom, I'm going to walk Telford back to his house," Aubrey said.

Ignatius and Merle worked together to clean up.

"Thank you so much, Ignatius," said Merle. "These old bones, you know."

"I find it curious that you grow old. You and Grandmom."

"Grandmom and I decided we would in stages... for Aubrey's sake. Until she has full knowledge we want her to be comfortable. As Grandmom said, tonight is a big night. Let's see what Aubrey has to report tomorrow."

When she returned to the garden, Ignatius was back to himself. He and Merle had the yard cleaned up and everything put away.

"Your snow globe is on the kitchen table," Merle announced.

"Thanks for everything, you two!"

Before going upstairs, Aubrey made sure to put out a piece of the sandwich and a small cup of wine for Ignatius. He was out of sight, but near to be sure.

Merle lumbered off to bed carrying a glass and a bottle with the last of the wine.

As Aubrey settled in for a good night's sleep, Grandmom entered the Flora Room.

"Grandmom, it seemed like tonight's celebration was all about me."

"As it should be. Let me show you a little trick I learned on my twenty-third birthday." She placed a bright green candle next to the fairy globe on Aubrey's nightstand. As she lit it, Grandmom said, "Gaze into the flame with an open heart and say 'I honor you'."

Aubrey did so without question.

Grandmom placed jasmine on Aubrey's pillow. "This will help you sleep."

"Thank you, Grandmom. It is obvious that you are trying to take away my anxiety." Aubrey closed her eyes, slowly drifting into a peaceful sleep.

"I remember twenty-three. You will come to understand many things. This is the beginning of a brand new time. I've been hiding this world from you. But you are finally ready. This year will not be ruled by the same understood and agreeable laws set by common man. Tonight, dear Aubrey, our great Queen Mab will grace you. She is powerful. She is sovereign. As you accept her in slumber our fairyland will open its gates. Queen Mab knows a pure heart from a doubting one. Tonight, she will give birth to reality, in her way. Tomorrow, you will feel renewed. I am certain you will embrace your new life."

"But Grandmom…"

"Sleep, my sweet Aubrey. Sleep and dream." Grandmom shook the fairy globe. Wise boy, she thought. She gazed into the candle flame and said,

"Great Mab please take Aubrey through the thin lines of separation. Tonight she is poised between light and dark. On this Autumn Equinox the veil is thinnest. Take her to a land that vibrates in a different rhythm. In your way, provide guidance."

"I've been waiting for you," came a voice from above.

Aubrey looked up, shielding her eyes from the sun's streaming rays.

"Up here, in the Elder tree." There was a pause. "You look nicer that way," said the same voice.

"What do you mean?" asked Aubrey, frustrated that she could not see.

"Well, a shimmering green dress appears to suit you. This will be your new look. Queen Mab has chosen an emerald headband woven with silver threads, as well. Your shoes are a bit too fancy for my taste. But feel lucky to have this look chosen for you. Being only a half fairy, you seem to have a great deal of pull. Most fairies find their look. You however, were given yours within this peaceful dream. Because you are from above, I will call you Star."

"But my name is Aubrey."

"Ah, yes, Aubrey. That means Elf Ruler. Perhaps a profession left for your future. I've heard you're unemployed, at present. Queen Mab and Grandmom have ordered me to be of meaningful instruction, a tour guide if you will."

"Who are you?"

"The name's Tara. I am a descendent of the Land of Thornewood. Seems I'm destined to watch from above. Which is ironic because I come from below. Who knew?"

"Can you come down so we might talk face to face?"

The scent of jasmine lingered in the air, and the garden was brighter than in previous days. It reminded her of childhood, and being able to water the beautiful Foxglove, Laurel, and Moonseed plants.

"Oh, hang on. The Queen didn't tell me you would be so needy." Quickly, in two fleeting descents, Tara landed on the path before Aubrey.

"You don't look like a fairy that I remember from my childhood stories. You're clothes are drab, and there is no sparkle to you at all. My apologies, but you appear to be a bit rough about the edges."

"How could I zip up and down, in and out, all about the trees in the garden wearing a fancy, sparkling gown? I'm more like a soldier. All fairies have a purpose. Mine is to protect from above. I didn't think sparkles and a flowery wreath around my head would provide the best camouflage. Anyone with second sight might see shiny stuff in a tree. I take care of things. Make sense?"

"What is second sight?"

"That's when a mortal, or half mortal is granted the ability to see magical folk. You were granted second sight by Grandmom."

"I see. But, I don't mean for you to take care of me. My grandmother and I take care of each other. You seem to know her."

"Yes, I know Grandmom. She and Queen Mab are like this." Tara crossed two fingers on her right hand. "Any way, you're with me until you wake up. Think about it, Star. You fell asleep being placed in a typical fairy trance. Grandmom knows what she's doing. It was quick and did the trick. Hey, I rhymed!"

Not amused, Aubrey responded, "I suppose it does. Are you up in the tree all of the time. In stories, I thought fairies lived below the ground, and came up at certain times. And why is it sunny?"

"This might not make sense, but right now we are below the ground. The garden you see before you is really a more beautiful version of the same garden above."

Aubrey watched as Tara pulled an arrow from a sheath on her back. A bow appeared in the very next second. Tara wielded the arrow toward the greenhouse. As quickly as it flew, Tara leapt and retrieved it midair. "I shoot at things that need to be shot. I protect things that are clueless. I see everything, boring and otherwise in the garden. That is my job."

"Did you see Patty and I painting the wishing well?"

"Better than that, I saw that horrible Jack hit Patty... more than a few times."

"Surely you could have shot him. Not that I'm joining in the suicide versus homicide dispute."

"Killing him was not my job. Between Grandmom and the Queen my orders get sent to me. I follow them, and ask no questions."

"Can you tell me why I'm dressed like this?"

"Finally something easy. You are in your astral body. That is when you are able to visit this world. And because you are half-fairy, or as we prefer to be called Fair Folk, it is fitting that you be the true you while you're here. You've always been a half-fairy. However, Grandmom has decided that your twenty third birthday be a celebration of the great announcement. Both she and Queen Mab have decided it's time for you to embrace it and cross over."

"Am I a Fair Folk when I'm not here?"

"Absolutely. And your powers will be used in the coming months. For the rest of your life, really. You'll discover what they are as the days pass. This is sort of like your initiation. From now on you will not need to pass into this world through your dreams. But because you are only half-fairy, you do not get a free ticket to come and go. There are certain offerings that you will need to know about. I will give you a special token to make your travels safe."

"What do you mean?"

"All Fair Folk gather in a group called a gentry. Our gentry is very small; Malvina, a few others, and me. You've met Merle and Ignatius. Just for sport I'm leaving a few names out for now."

"Mystery and questions are becoming quite familiar to me, so I won't hold it against you. Hey is Merle a half fairy like me?"

"No, he's a Satyr. Most Satyrs are great musicians and can play the panpipe. He played it at your party. Queen Mab has the power to grant special privileges to anyone. For instance a Satyr is not the prettiest of magical folk. Merle has the ability to look like a human man all the time. Sure he can change back, too. Satyrs don't usually live in families like humans, but I think Merle has a soft spot for Grandmom."

"Is that possible?"

"That's what I love about newbies coming for a visit during their astral time... you don't overreact or get all worked up about too much."

"So let's get back to how I can be a part of this world if I need to. And would I like Malvina?"

"Oh, sure you would. But Malvina is off limits. She is a fairy of gentle spirit, and very different than other members of our gentry. Anyway, I'm going to make this easy on you."

Tara pulled a necklace from a pouch around her waist. On it hung a tiny hourglass filled with black glitter. "Here hold this. You will use it to move from one world to the other. When I say 'now' tip it, then tip it right back. You'll see yourself sleeping, then back here to me. Easy right?"

Before Aubrey had a chance to take it in, Tara shouted, "Now!" All at once Aubrey was back in her room, tipped the hourglass, and was right back to Tara in the garden.

"Oh, my!" said Aubrey.

"That hourglass has passed through the hands of many

folk. Some were magical, some were ghosts. It last belonged to a young girl named Anna Thorne. She loved the gardens of Thornewood Castle in a place called Washington. After she died, her ghost visited the fairies of the castle's gardens. It was then she discovered one of the fairies had taken her necklace from her jewelry box. When she found this out she made the fairy and all the fairies thereafter promise to give it as a gift for the next hundred years. Or else tragedy would prevail. Ghosts are tricky like that I guess."

"I will wear it and use its powers wisely. Will there be a time when I should give it as a gift, just as you did?"

"Yes, but that time will come naturally. You don't need to worry about it."

"Thank you for this."

"One last thing. To come into this world and call upon your fairy magic, you must be standing directly on a ley line."

"What is that?"

"A ley line is a path. There is a subtle energy. This is where our world vibrates in a different rhythm than the world of humans. The veil is thin and travel is possible. You must stand on a ley line, then turn the hourglass."

"How will I know how to find a ley line?"

"There are only three nearby. They are drawn here in the garden between the trees. From the Pine to the Elder, from the Elder to the Hawthorn, from the Hawthorn to the Pine. It creates a triangle. If Queen Mab and Grandmom tell me to, I will give you more information. For now you have it pretty easy."

Aubrey fumbled with the hourglass on the chain around her neck, then quickly let it go. "Oh, I'll be more careful," Aubrey said.

"No, no, don't worry. It doesn't work like that. You can't move from one world to the other unless you want to. There are no accidents in our gentry. We do everything with imposing purpose, and with the guidance of our leaders."

"Who are our leaders?"

"Lady Bhaltair and the Great Queen Mab."

"Will I feel differently when I wake up?"

"You will still be you, but half-fairies have a big responsibility. You must always be on the look out for liars, cheaters, and people who want to hurt other humans. In our underworld we all just keep to ourselves unless we are summoned. For example, by order of Grandmom, I am to be your guide. At times you will be confused. Remember you are not alone. As a gentry we can make all worlds better."

"Are you saying that I will be able to see more clearly who and what a human is?"

"Yes, you will. Especially with your second sight."

"Explain that again."

"It means you have the ability, at any time, to tell a Halfling from a pure human. You can also spot a changeling. A changeling is a magical creature that is trying to look human. This is where it gets fun, and as time goes by you'll be able to control it. For instance, as I said, Merle is a Satyr. The next time you see him, don't be alarmed. His true self may fade in and out. Also, be careful in using your second sight. Some fairies are really devils that may lead you astray. There are exceptions."

"What is that?"

"For example, if a magical being has made a pact with the real devil of the human world, it is possible that second sight is powerless."

"This is such a great deal of information. Don't get me wrong, I am very grateful, but yesterday it was just a simple birthday. It must be morning by now."

"Oh, you are very new at this. Time can be controlled. I chose for time to stand still. You will be very rested when you wake up. Flip the hourglass." Tara leapt to the Elder tree and shouted back, "Until we meet again, my new friend, Star."

SEPTEMBER 24

Aubrey woke the next morning, refreshed as promised. The necklace was on the nightstand next to Telford's gift. She noticed how different Tara was from the fairy sitting in the globe. Her fictional fairy was dressed in a beautiful skirt made of leaves and a top fashioned from flowers. At once, she felt beneath the covers. Just an old pair of pajamas. No shimmering dress. There was no emerald band around her forehead. But she knew dreams like hers came only to the enchanted. Upon rising she felt lighter, free of worry. After getting dressed she put on the hourglass necklace, shook the fairy globe, and hurried off to find Grandmom, Merle, and Ignatius.

"Oh, Grandmom this has been the most wonderful birthday of all. Was your twenty-third just the same?"

"Not exactly. I am glad you are pleased, however."

"Can you tell me more about Tara?"

"If you wish. Tara is a helpful fairy. She sticks to herself, and does not like the introduction of anything new. Her main role, in our gentry, is to protect the garden. Sharp weapons are her specialty. I call upon her when I need another set of hands. Her recent task was to bestow onto you the hourglass."

"Can you tell me more about it?"

"Over a century ago a sizable manor was built on the west coast. It was considered a home of great reputation. The parapet on one side granted it the stature of castle. When the owner of the castle died in 1954 he left it to his daughter Anna. For many of her younger years she peered out her bedroom window watching the festivities in the gardens below. At birth she had suffered severe hearing loss, and the aids that she wore brought great ridicule from the staff, their children, and her school friends, as they were. Her only companion was a fairy, our very own feisty Tara. Together they would observe the grand parties, making up stories of their own wearing ball gowns and beautiful jewelry. Their late evening visits to the garden brought such joy to Anna. By the time of her death, Anna was able to name all of the flowers in the grand garden. Tara loved her so. It was told that Anna died in her sleep, but to Tara, Anna's death was a mystery. Castle history promotes stories of hauntings along its great hallways and within the walls of many rooms. Tara has admitted that Anna's death made her restless, and thought answers would bring peace to both Tara's mind and Anna's soul. Our great Queen Mab did not like that Tara spent most of her time toiling away with this mystery. We have our Queen to thank for sending Tara to us. Queen Mab thought Tara would prosper in a new, yet much smaller garden, focusing on the living and not the dead. When Tara arrived she was filled with angst. Her new home was not to her liking, and she had no one. I noticed that she found comfort living within the trees. I asked Tara what she would like to do. She wanted, most of all, to watch from above, just as she had at Thornewood Castle. Now Tara is our lookout, if you will. She has an arsenal of arrows, darts, daggers, and poison tipped twigs. Her best weapon above all is the ability to know the pulse of the garden. It was Tara that knew about the unrest between that couple, Patty and Jack, before the rest of us. It was Tara that keeps the nosey ones out. While Telford may be harmless, he is quite an articulate young lad with a sharp mind… ready to share a story. He is, to be sure, a friend to keep close."

"Do you think Tara is happy here at the inn?"

"The mystery of Anna's death has toughened this once gentle fairy. But it is to our advantage. I have spoken with Queen Mab, and we agreed that the happenings of Thornewood Castle are unfair, yet solvable. At just the precise time we will take Tara back to uncover the unknown. Tara is aware of this promise. In the meantime she puts a great deal of serious ambition into her role here at The Petit Jardin."

SEPTEMBER 25

The next several days were filled with hope for Aubrey. She woke each morning with a lightness of air. Talks with Grandmom and Merle became less like riddles. So this is what it feels like to be part of a gentry, she thought. She would shake the fairy globe, put on her necklace, and plan each day. Merle's true self did fade in and out, just as Tara had foretold. There were no uncomfortable feelings, only a nod of the head now and then. Ignatius was intrigued by her. He, Grandmom, and Merle were pure magical beings. Each could transform, among other things. That's how Ignatius was able to come to the party and be in Aubrey's life. Telford knew nothing of ley lines or second sight. Grandmom made quite sure that he was never exposed to the magical world. He remained innocent of heart. Just as Tara helped Aubrey, Aubrey would one day help Telford. Telford's mom Laura was a Halfling. While her life in Ste. Germaine was spent selling saddles, she was eyes and ears for Queen Mab and Grandmom. In return they granted her small wishes here and there. The most recent wish was that Telford have a friend. She continually asked that he not ever be exposed to the gentry in its true form, but Queen Mab would not hear of it. "We are proud of who we are," she would say. "If you are ashamed, then you are not one of us." This would infuriate Laura, but she understood the inevitableness of the fairy world. Telford could not remain sheltered forever. Grandmom felt otherwise.

Aubrey enjoyed breakfast that morning. Merle made a fare of biscuits and gravy with cantaloupe. "I have been given a new name, Grandmom."

"Tara is good for that."

"Has she given you a name?"

"Of course she has. She is the one who named me Grandmom. I, however, prefer to be called Miss Nola Bhaltair."

"What about you, Merle? Has she given you a name?"

"No," responded Merle as he began to clear the table. "We have a strictly professional relationship."

Aubrey helped Merle. When the task was complete she faced Grandmom who was reading the newspaper and sipping her tea.

"I think I'll set about to look for a job today."

"What on earth for, my dear?"

"I'm staying here for free, eating for free, and not doing very much of anything. Having a job will make me feel like I'm contributing. Most of all, I love to be with people."

"Well, I certainly do not think it is necessary, but if you must, I will support you. What might you like to spend your time doing?"

"Isn't there a garden shop here in Ste. Germaine? My education and experience might get me on there."

Merle spoke up. "Yes, there is. It is called Crabapple Corner. They're located just about a mile north, where Main Street turns into Little Rock Road. You'll see it right away, as there isn't much else out that way. Telford's mom works out that way. Oh, and you'll get a nice view of the Mississippi River. I know the folks that run the place. They were very helpful when I wanted to get the greenhouse started. It might not look like it, but I do care about the garden. I'll call ahead if you like."

"That would be wonderful, Merle. Thanks. I'll get changed and head on over."

Merle left the kitchen to make the call. Aubrey quickly finished the dishes.

"You are very good to him, my dear," Grandmom said.

Hoping to make a good first impression, Aubrey selected her best business casual. She chose her favorite khakis and a powder blue shirt. Brown loafers and a brown belt finished the ensemble. She tied her long blonde hair back with a matching blue ribbon. Her dangling silver hoops were traded in for small post earrings. Instinctively, she reached for the hourglass dangling around her neck. It made her feel strong and safe.

Aubrey stopped to wash her car at the Speedy Clean. She was looking forward to having a purpose. Helping around the inn when she was young was just a pretend job. The boarding school would not allow the students to have work. Grandmom saw to it that her bank account had a consistent and meager amount. She worked at the Missouri Botanical Garden without Grandmom's blessing. Just enough to get by, her grandmother would say. Concentrating on good grades was to be her focus.

She pulled into Crabapple Corner and parked near the hay bales between two of the buildings.

"There she is," shouted a woman from the large red building. "Come look, Martin, it's little Aubrey Bhaltair all grown up. She showed up just like Merle said she would."

Aubrey did not remember these two from her time in Ste. Germaine so very long ago.

"Let's have a look at you. I'm Betty and this is my husband, Martin. We've gotten on a little bit since you were here last, but we're still able to outfit this small town with the most beautiful flowers this side of the Mississippi River. Isn't that right, Martin?"

"It's very nice to meet you both," Aubrey responded as she shook their hands in turn. "Did Merle tell you that I'd like to apply for a job, if that's possible?"

"He sure did. Now you know winter is coming so things will slow down, but we could sure use part-time help until the spring. There are a lot of little things to do, including errands. Merle said you're a hard worker. Do you think part-time will work for you?"

"Of course, part-time will be great. I've been trying to get Merle to let me do more chores around the inn."

"That Merle is a stubborn one. It's awfully nice of you to help him out. And he'll be the last one to admit he's not getting any younger. That inn means the world to him. A while back, we asked about the garden. He was a little embarrassed about it. So we offered to give it a small makeover. He said he was waiting for just the right time, and just the right person. I guess that must be you, huh?"

"I do have some ideas."

"Well, working for us will get you a fifteen percent discount. Can you start tomorrow? We need to create a daily to-do list for you. That way we all stay out of each other's hair."

"I would love to start tomorrow. Will jeans and a t-shirt be okay?"

"Nothing any fancier than that. Come around eleven. Martin is the cook around here. He'll fix us up a simple lunch and we'll go over some of the details. You didn't ask how much we pay."

"No, I suppose I didn't. How much is it?"

"Down at Ace Hardware's garden department they pay

nine dollars and ninety cents an hour. There's a fancy place down in Cape Girardeau called The Flower Box. I have it on good authority that they pay fifteen dollars. How about we split the difference. Does thirteen dollars an hour to start sound okay?"

"That will work just fine for me. See you both at eleven o'clock tomorrow. I won't disappoint you!"

Aubrey sat in her car for a moment, soaking it all in. There were three buildings. The large metal one seemed more for storage. It had huge doublewide doors that were open and no windows. She could see a tractor and an inventory of hay. A second one was red with white trim around its windows. It was for the customers to come and go, shop, and pay. The third building was more of a greenhouse. The thick plastic walls bellowed gently with the blowing wind. There were purposeful holes in the plastic roof. From her job at the Missouri Botanical Gardens, Aubrey knew the environment had to be just right to provide flowers the best chance of a healthy life. Out of the corner of her eye she saw the selection of concrete yard decorations between two of the buildings. How, ironic she thought, when she saw the fairy statue. It stood about two feet tall, had wings, and was holding a bowl. That must be for birds to drink water. It was lovely. Though made of stone, it was a happy fairy indeed. She would certainly not need fifteen percent off that, for she had her very own fairy in the garden at the inn.

Merle texted to ask how it had gone. She answered and sat parked on the lot for a few minutes more. It would be a nice place to work. She looked forward to the customer service, running errands, and working quietly with the flowers and bushes. She was very grateful to Merle for making the call. Martin and Betty seemed like good hometown people. Normal is good, she thought with a smile.

Back at the inn, Grandmom greeted Aubrey at the door. "Merle tells me things went well. Most cannot find work so easily. But they are good people and are lucky to have you. I'm sure you know what's best for you, but I am going to miss having you underfoot all day."

"Thank you, Grandmom. If it's okay, I'd like to start work on the garden today. First, I'm going to draw up some diagrams. A landscaper always begins with a plan. I'll run them by you for approval. Martin and Betty said I could have fifteen percent off any purchase from their garden shop. Plus I'll do all the labor."

"That is all very nice, my dear. I'm okay with you planting, raking, and such. But you may not pay for anything. The garden belongs to the inn and the inn will pay for the beautification you are bringing to its grounds. As for approval, please consider Merle. I will enjoy looking at the plans, as well. I'm sure they will be delightful. One condition, however."

"And what is that, Grandmom?"

"You may add to the garden, but you may not take away or rearrange. The set up, as it is, is quite important to the soul of the garden. You do understand, I'm sure."

"Yes, of course, Grandmom."

As Aubrey went upstairs to get her sketchpad, her mind drifted to the astral encounter she had with Tara. Tara, she knew, was part of the soul of the garden. It didn't seem necessary to Aubrey that she and her grandmother continue to speak in riddles. But she would do things in a manner to Grandmom's liking. She retrieved the sketchpad and pencils from her closet and headed down a narrow staircase between the Foxglove and Flora rooms. It led directly to the garden. The floorboards at the bottom of the long narrow staircase creaked with each step. Just another thing that might use a little handyman help, she thought.

When she got to the garden, Merle was coming from the greenhouse. "Can I see inside?"

"Not yet, Aubrey."

She smiled. "It doesn't hurt to ask."

"What's the paper for?"

"I'd like to sketch out some ideas I have for the garden. I'd love to get your input."

"That would be alright."

"I'm a bit distracted by the metal bistro set. Would it be

alright if I used the rest of the white paint to give it a touch up?"

"Sure. You know where the supplies are. And you did a fine job cleaning the brushes last time. Don't forget to use the tarp. So you don't get paint on the grass. The mowers won't be returning for the rest of the season."

"Thanks, Merle."

Aubrey headed toward the shed for the supplies.

"Hey Aubrey," called Telford from the side lot. "Whatcha' doin'?"

"Getting ready to paint the table and chair set in the garden. Want to help?"

"Sure."

"Hey, I've never seen you wear that necklace. Is it new?"

"Yes, a friend named Tara gave it to me."

"Cool!"

"I found this sandpaper in the shed. It's probably a good idea to smooth down some of the rough spots before we paint. Here's a piece for you."

After the sanding was finished, they lifted each piece of the weather worn metal bistro set and placed them one at a time on the tarp.

"These two brushes should work. Have you ever painted something like this before?"

"No, I'm pretty good with a hammer, though."

"That might come in handy if we build something in the garden. And I haven't forgotten about your being an expert with a shovel, as well."

They both smiled. Aubrey demonstrated a few times how to dip the brush, then scrape off the excess paint on the inside of the can.

"This is fun business, Aubrey."

"Doing things with a friend is always fun. Hey, I've got some news."

"What's that?"

"I got a job today… at Crabapple Corner. I'm meeting with the owners again tomorrow to go over details."

"Does that mean we'll see less of each other?"

"Of course not. I'll only be part-time. You'll be at school while I'm at work. In the summer, when it gets busier, maybe you can do odd jobs for them. Summer is a long way off, but when the time is right I'll put in a good word for you."

"That would be great."

They finished the bistro set before dinner. It was time for Telford to head home.

"I'd like to meet your mom. When is a good time to visit?"

"She works quite a bit. But I'll ask her. Hey a house just went up for sale next to ours."

"Remind me again of your address."

"One ninety-eight Third Street. We're right across from the pewter store."

"I didn't notice it when I took you home on my birthday. What's the pewter store?"

"It's a shop for tourists, I guess. They make things like metal dishes and Christmas tree ornaments. It has a funny smell most of the time. I think they're always melting the pewter. My mom says it's kind of pricey, so we don't shop there. We don't really have anyone to buy presents for anyway. They do have wind chimes. Maybe the garden could use a new set."

"That's a perfect idea. The nursery might have wind chimes, as well. Time for you to get going. I'll clean up here. Tell your mom what I said about meeting her. And Telford, I can't tell you how much I love the special gift you gave to me."

"I'm really happy! See ya'."

Aubrey cleaned the brushes and put all of the supplies back into the shed. She settled on the thinking bench and opened her sketchpad. In her diagram she began with the greenhouse. Her curiosity almost got the best of her. The number padlock and her respect for Merle swayed her. Hopefully it was just a normal greenhouse with no magical surprises. It would be great, she thought, to be able to use it when spring came and she could start grooming the garden.

After helping with dinner and the dishes, Aubrey retired

to her room. She wanted to get out a few of her textbooks from college. It would be nice if Martin and Betty could benefit from her knowledge. Brushing up didn't seem like a bad idea. As a habit, she took off her necklace and put it on the nightstand next to the fairy globe. After her shower she set her alarm, then climbed into bed with her 'America's Garden Book'. It was one of her favorite texts, containing over eight hundred pages on anything and everything that could be grown. She especially loved the diagrams that illustrated necessary planting dimensions. There were sections on what the names of flowers meant, and how to cure plant diseases. Her professor chose it because it had been edited by the New York Botanical Garden. He called it a respected bible in the business of horticulture.

A few hours had passed. Enough for tonight, she thought. The large queen-size bed left plenty of room for the book and her. She drifted off to sleep, looking forward to her first day of work.

SEPTEMBER 26

When her alarm went off at eight o'clock she woke easily and with a smile on her face. She didn't have any feelings that fairies had poked around inside her head the last few evenings. When, she wondered, would she turn the hourglass in the garden? Why would she need to?

Aubrey had decided that she would not be wearing the hourglass necklace to work. Her time at The Missouri Botanical Garden taught her that dangling objects could certainly get in the way while toting, digging, and planting. She would be heartsick if anything happened to it or worse yet, if it were to fall off without her knowing. It would be safe next to the globe, she thought.

Aubrey loved having a job where sensible clothes were expected. She decided new shoes or boots might be in order after she found out what her duties would be.

"Breakfast was wonderful, Merle."

"Thank you, Aubrey."

Debbie Nuessle

"Oh, Merle."

"Yes?"

"I've been meaning to apologize to you for lying about my name, saying it was Bree."

"I was not offended. Coming back here took courage, I know. It was only natural for you to be a little suspicious. Funny I haven't apologized to you for not telling you that I'm a Satyr."

This made them both laugh.

"By the way, where's Grandmom?"

"When she didn't come down, I sent her a note up through the dumb waiter. The privacy of texting cannot always be trusted. She wrote back saying she wasn't feeling well. I sent a plate back up. I suspect we'll see her this evening. Sometimes 'not feeling well' really means there's something in the air."

"How do you mean?"

"Grandmom can sense when the gentry needs to be summoned."

"That doesn't sound like my cup of tea."

"Make no mistake, Aubrey, you are now part of the gentry. For good and for bad."

Aubrey cleared her place and went upstairs for her purse, jacket, and sunglasses. She left through the front door and made a right to the side parking lot. Her beloved Volkswagen TSI was not used to sitting out in the elements. A garage space was included with the rent of her small apartment. She was not looking forward to scraping snow during the winter months.

It was too early to go to work. Her plan was to drive up and down a few streets, getting reacquainted with good old Ste. Germaine. First point of interest would be Telford's house. Making a left out of the inn's lot, she remembered two blocks down Main, a right on Market, then a left on Third. Directions were spot on and she ended up on Telford's street. She found the pewter shop. It was called Ye Olde Melting Pot, appropriately. Directly across was a quaint home with a postage stamp front yard. The curtains in the window were tied with ribbons, and the front porch was decorated nicely for Halloween. Her mind wandered. Was Telford too old to wear a costume? Did the inn hand out candy? Then there's the matter of having fairies on the property. Oh, my!

Just as Telford had said, the house next door was for sale. It was fashioned like the rest of the homes on the block, but very run down. How would it ever sell?

She headed up and down a few more streets. She noticed a new wine seller on Market Street. That would be a great suggestion for couples that might stay at the inn. She thought about Patty, hoping all was well. The dashboard clock read 10:45. Time to head to work. That had a great ring to it, she thought.

"Where would you like me to park each day? I don't want my car taking up space or getting in the way of your customers."

"First of all, 'our' customers," responded Betty. "And behind the storage shed will do just fine. If you need to run errands you're to use our truck." Betty pointed to the old Ford pick-up truck in front of the garden store. "It can haul just about anything. Come on in, lunch is waiting. Martin decided to let someone else do the cooking. There's a place just up from Annabelle's."

"Best burgers in town," said Martin. "The Ste. Germaine Diner. Been in business since 1978. Everything is fresh and made-to-order. You will not be disappointed."

"That was nice of you to pick up lunch. I'd love to pay for mine."

"Absolutely not. Betty and I teased about this earlier. We're going to write this off as a company power lunch! We're glad you're here, and think good things are going to come of this for all of us."

"I feel the same way."

Martin and Betty turned out to be slow talkers and even slower eaters. It took a while to get down to the nuts and bolts of Aubrey's new job. But when it did she was very pleased. Her hours were nine to twelve, Tuesday through Thursday. During their slow time, duties included washing and sorting planting pots, keeping the store organized, sweeping, and running daily errands.

"Do you know anything about computers?" Betty asked.

"I know some. What did you have in mind?"

"We thought it might be time for one of those fancy web pages. It might help business."

"I've never built a website before, but I guess I can learn."

"Could there be a class at the library?"

"I'm sure there is. Or I might be able to learn online."

"If you look into that, let us know. We'll pay for the class."

"That sounds great. By the way, Betty."

"What's that?"

"Where should I put my purse when I come in each day. Being from St. Louis, as a habit, it's not a good idea to leave a purse in your car."

"Of course not. Even the small town of Ste. Germaine has its worries. Let me show you a safe place in the office."

They walked to a second smaller room connected to the office. Along with a very old desk, there were file cabinets, a few old office chairs, and a small table.

"We have what you might call, meetings in here. Right here in the bottom drawer is a good place to put your purse. I keep mine in the top one. Feel free to have your cell phone while working. You never know when you might need it to call a supplier, or check on something."

"That's good to know. Even being aware of the local weather might come in handy at a garden shop. Don't you think?"

"You are absolutely right."

"Oh, I forgot to ask. Do I clock in or sign a card? How will you know how many hours I've worked?"

"I told Martin he needed to come up with a system. Sometimes he can be so forgetful. On the other hand, we've never had anyone work for us before."

"How about if I come up with a form, and make some copies of it?"

"Sounds like a good idea. You're not even on the clock yet,

and you're more than earning your keep."

"Betty, I am so grateful for this opportunity. Please be honest with me, if I'm doing something wrong."

"Honey, you know you're smart enough to make more money doing what you love somewhere else. For some reason you came back to Ste. Germaine. Martin and I are so happy that dear old Merle brought us together. I have a good feeling about this. Hopefully you won't be too bored during these next few months. Things will be kind of slow for a short while. It will liven up a bit at Christmas. And come spring, things will get to hoppin'. You talents will be used a bit more. We'll see you on Tuesday."

"You and Martin are such sweet people. I don't know if I should hug you or shake your hand."

"Ah, hugs are best."

Aubrey headed around to her car. She checked her phone wondering if there would be a text from Merle. Nothing. The garden lot exited onto the narrow Little Rock Road. With a sloping hill to the left, yielding was necessary. Coming over the crest was a large truck. As it passed by, Aubrey read 'The Move's On Us' on the side of the truck. She followed it toward town. They parted ways at the intersection of Washington and Main.

When she arrived back at the inn, Aubrey was greeted at the front door by Merle.
He said, "Grandmom's calling a meeting tonight. You'll be needing you're necklace, and I see you're not wearing it."

"The necklace is too special to wear to work. And why will I need it?"

Merle paused..."Our meeting is with the gentry in the garden. Grandmom will be in her room until that time. I'll order a pizza. No dishes or cleanup."

Aubrey remembered learning that the gentry simply meant a group of fair folk and other creatures that banned together as a small community. While she was honored to be included in the gentry, she had reservations.

"Merle, should I be frightened?"

"Were you frightened on your birthday?"

"Of course not. It was a wonderful celebration."

"No, I mean later that evening, in your dreams. Were you frightened then? And were you frightened when you first met Ignatius?"

"No, as a matter of fact, neither of those times upset me. Both occasions seemed to happen naturally. Will I meet anyone new this evening? Tara told me about a fairy named Malvina."

"Grandmom usually does not involve Malvina. She is very quiet and extremely shy. In addition, she has her own important duties to attend to."

They heard movement from the dumbwaiter.

"Grandmom has sent a note. This evening, we are to meet on the ley line that runs between the Hawthorne and the Pine."

Later, at dinner, Merle tried to make small talk to put Aubrey at ease. Finally, Merle stood up. Aubrey reached for the hourglass that rested on her sweater, and quietly followed him to the garden. Ignatius was there. They watched as Grandmom came from the side door to join them.

"Good, you're all here. This is of utmost importance. After our journey we will arrive at a spring near the base of the Hawthorn tree. There must be complete silence. It is especially important, Aubrey, that you are seen and not heard. You are a newcomer to the other world, and impressions can be made quickly. Citizens there are kind in nature, but quick to judge. And their judgment is most times done silently. There is no benefit of the doubt where we are going. Your only duty is to turn the hourglass when I place my hand upon your shoulder. Do you understand?"

"I do."

"Gather in close. Ignatius, you stand on the other side of Aubrey. Tara, do come down from that tree this moment."

"I thought you'd never ask. A fairy can get a complex, you know." She continued, "Hey, Star... pretty cool, huh."

"Do be silent, Tara," Grandmom insisted.

Grandmom stood in the middle, and the four of them

joined hands in a circle around her. The night air turned to a chill, and frost was forming on patches of grass.
She began,

"Now's the time, the time's again
To join the world, the world within
Welcome us with hearts so pure
Pull us in if you are sure
We seek to take this magical quest
The world within can guide us best
Through the lines that stand between
Bring us in to meet our Queen."

With that, Grandmom put her hand upon Aubrey's shoulder. The hourglass was turned as instructed. With the other hand she held tightly to Ignatius' hand. At once, however, she found that each of them were sitting on oddly shaped stones, next to a turquoise blue body of water. A mist hovered a few inches above the ground. There was brilliant moonlight overhead, and it formed a sparkling layer on top of the water. Suddenly, a woman, no a fairy, rose from the water. Her gown was a shimmering white, and her hair was golden. A silver dagger hung from a belt around her waist. On a hillock behind her stood a gathering of fairies. There must have been a few dozen, or even more. They swayed in unison, and their glistening wings seemed to bend to the rhythm of a gentle breeze. The great fairy floated slowly toward the gentry.

Aubrey reached for Ignatius. But he shook his head with meaning. She wondered... if she turned the hourglass, could she escape this?

The woman spoke... "Lady Bhaltair, you performed a magnificent gathering chant, as always. And I see you've brought the newest addition to your gentry. Please introduce. Leave out no details. Who is she and what does she know? And most importantly, how can she be an asset?"

Grandmom stood and began to speak. "Greetings, good

Queen Mab. This is my granddaughter, Aubrey Bhaltair. Her magic is fueled by her half-fairy soul. She has yet to discover what her powers might be. At present, she is under the guidance of Tara, our trusted guard. In earthly matters, Merle is her tutor. Ignatius provides her with wit and friendship."

Tara, Merle, and Ignatius stood, bowed slightly, then sat back down.

"I see. And what about the young boy she has been seen with? Danger may befall him if he gets too close to your gentry. Can we agree on this?" Queen Mab stared directly at Aubrey.

"We will be diligent in his protection," Grandmom answered.

"Very well. Let's tend to the business at hand. Important news has come to me from England. Your town is in grave danger. All fair folk and magical beings in Ste. Germaine may fall to their death by the hand of evil. Wild Edric of Wales, considered a demon in our magical world, has managed to conquer a rebirth, if you will. His mission is to destroy the magical populace one small town at a time. News has spread that three gentries in greater London were destroyed. Not a trace is left. I should have been consulted at the onset, but no one knew how powerful and inclusive the killings would be. In America, he is starting with Ste. Germaine, and our job is to stop him. Of course, I must be protected. The underworld of this town is relying on you to put an end to his reign of terror. He is alone, but has great stealth and defenses. What you think may work on a mere mortal, will not work on him. He is a Dark Elf. That may work to your advantage. His arrogance brings confidence. Does he have second sight? This remains to be seen. Be on guard at every minute."

Grandmom spoke, "May I ask, is his motive known?"

"Wild Edric, born of England, acquired, with force, a fairy wife. Her sisters watched without recourse as Lady Godda was taken away. A prenuptial was established. Edric was never to speak of his wife's past or her sisters. One evening, after a long hunt, he arrived home and could not find Lady Godda. He called out to her, and when she appeared, he accused her of being with her sisters in his absence. The pledge had been broken, and he never saw his fairy bride again. To make matters worse, his fortune dwindled. He mourned for days and nights. Weak from grief, he died. As he was about to enter the other world where the human God exists, the Devil held out his hand. Wild Edric, in exchange for his soul, asked to be a henchman for the Devil. There are many kinds to choose from in the shopping cart of doom. Wild Edric most wanted to be a Dark Elf. He thought this suited his plan for revenge. The Devil agreed, but wanted more. So Wild Edric, in trade for changeling powers, would send the souls of his prey to hell for the next fifty years. Edric was sure this was enough time to complete his plan of desolation. He abhors fairies and their unbreakable promises. So, with the Devil, he made a few of his own. To our advantage, we have a great number of allies. And he does not. He is motivated by hate, and we are motivated by love and what is right. Because of his changeling powers, he will most likely appear as a normal man, or perhaps even a woman. Dark Elves are most often handsome, so beware of his ability to charm. It is common knowledge that Dark Elves are taught the art of fighting and war. While not born a Dark Elf, the Devil has granted this particular member of the fiery underworld strength and cunning. You will never see him eat, lest he fools you. For his diet consists of lizards, rats, and insects. We have eyes and ears everywhere. This will not be the last summons. I will be out of sight until we meet again. If I were to die at his hands, the underworld would immediately cease to exist. Lady Bhaltair, I expect a finalized plan from you in the next few days."

"Yes, Queen Mab."

"One last thing. Aubrey Bhaltair, are you aware of the meaning your name holds?"

"I was told, but that seems so long ago."

"At its English origin it means Elf Ruler. This places great responsibility on your shoulders. Both your mother and grand-mother knew this twenty-three years ago. Many are counting on you and the power you can bring to this gentry. All of you, go at once. And do not disappoint!"

The great Queen Mab drifted back to the water. She lowered into the pond. The fairies that once stood on the small hill beyond the pond, were no more. Everyone in the gentry joined hands around Grandmom. She nodded at Aubrey, who knew what to do. Grandmom began to speak:

"Now's the time, the time's again
To leave this world, the world within
Send us back with ready hands
To fight the evil against our land
We'll summon the magic to serve us best
Until defeat we will not rest
Through the lines that once we stood
Take us back to the mortal world."

Grandmom placed her hand upon Aubrey's shoulder. The hourglass was turned, and once again they stood in the garden above. Aubrey fell to her knees and began to sob.

"Oh, Grandmom, this is too much for me. I'm sure I will fail. I am not a leader. My skill lies in being able to plant flowers, pull weeds, and trim hedges. Why have I been chosen? This is an impossible situation."

Ignatius helped her to her feet.

Grandmom spoke. "You are not alone. We are five against one because Dark Elves choose to work alone. They do so because they are arrogant. He has chosen to fight us in our world. They are quick to kill and slow to think. This is not my first encounter with a Dark Elf. As a gentry, our powers are greater than he will expect. In order for you to succeed you will need to believe in yourself, believe in our gentry. Until our next meeting, be aware of the town's happenings. He may already be lurking about. Remember, he is a changeling. Also, Queen Mab will be able to tell me more about this Dark Elf, his powers and his weaknesses. Your downfall, dear Aubrey, is your lack of confidence. This weakness will lessen your fairy powers."

"But Grandmom, I don't know what my powers are."

"One day, very soon, you will meet with Tara. Tara are you prepared?"

"Yes, Grandmom, I am certainly prepared to open her world."

The gentry dispersed for the evening.

SEPTEMBER 30

Tara began, "Don't be nervous. You need to draw on your ability to do what is right. You have been a kind person all your life. That is the energy you will need. What better person to save the fairy world than a kind and gentle half-fairy that puts others before herself?"

"I suppose that makes sense. However, I'm afraid that just because I'm nice doesn't necessarily make me strong."

"You are not required to have physical strength. Mental ability and a heart of gold will be part of your arsenal. Plus, you'll have a few tricks up your sleeve."

"I'm ready if you think I am."

"Come with me near the Elder tree. Yes. Now stand right here, on the path. When I touch your shoulder, turn your hourglass. Do not ever attempt to visit through these ley lines unless you are with someone. You may not enter this part of the underworld alone." Tara continued with a chant...

"Powers high and powers low
Weapons we need for one swift blow
Be it arrow or be it knife
Make its power take a life."

She put her hand on Aubrey's shoulder. Together they traveled softly to the underworld. On her last journey, Aubrey closed her eyes tightly as if falling into a dangerous and deep pool. Today she purposefully kept her eyes open. Within a few seconds, she saw the cloudy sky of daylight change to a starry night. Just as quickly, it changed into a brilliant sunlit time of day. Flowers everywhere. Marigolds, hibiscus, roses, and daisies. There were endless paths paved in brightly color stones. Birds seemed to be having clever and pleasant conversations.

"Why does this visit seem so different than our last one?" she asked Tara. "This land is more beautiful."

"Let me phrase it in a way you might understand. We took a different highway to another section of the underworld. Queen Mab only attends meetings at the Lake of Morality. That's where discussions are had about right and wrong, good and evil. It was necessary to meet there to discuss the Dark Elf. This particular section is the most sacred section. Secrets are kept here, that will one day be revealed. I am its sole protector. When I am not up in the Elder tree I am down here. To others it may seem like I'm toiling without purpose, but in reality I am standing watch and tending to one of the secrets."

"Is this where Malvina lives?"

"Yes, in fact, it is."

"Where is she? May I talk with her?"

"You may see her. But you may not speak to her. She is over there at the base of that tree."

"That looks exactly like our Elder tree."

"It is. You see, this world can mirror the one above for the purposes of we fair folk. Malvina is the keeper of the Elder tree in the underworld, and I am the keeper of all the garden's trees in the above world."

Aubrey saw a fairy with periwinkle wings and a shimmering pale blue dress. She was kneeling at the base of the Elder tree. Her hands were settled upon a tangerine colored mushroom with glistening white spots. The mossy grass around her tiny legs and bare feet was a deep lime green. She was facing away from them and seemed to be looking down to the base of the tree. Aubrey longed to talk to her. She began to call out her name. But Tara had foreseen Aubrey's foolishness and spun her around by the arm.

"Remember, you may not speak to Malvina. Her job is as constant as it is serious. I have brought you here to give you your weapon."

Aubrey was both startled and hurt. "Very well. Is it far from here?"

"No. Follow me."

Down a colored stone path they went in the opposite direction of the Elder tree. Aubrey took chances to look back as Malvina faded out of sight.

"Here we are," announced Tara at last. "This chest belongs to you."

"It seems quite large," reported Aubrey.

"Well of course it is. It holds the complete collection of your magical influence. This box has been under my watch for twenty-three years."

"I must have a great many powers!"

"You do, but you might be surprised to find what's inside."

"Tara, you and everyone else in the gentry always seem to keep me guessing."

"Go ahead and open it."

Aubrey approached the large chest. The top of its lid came up to her waist. Its size was the same in depth, length, and height. The sides were wooden and the top, stitched in leather, was covered in glitter. Tara blew a bit on the dust, and sparkles filled the air.

"Is that…?" Aubrey began to ask.

"Yes, of course it is. Fairy dust is not a myth. It exists at all the proper times."

Aubrey closed her eyes and took a deep breath. At once the brass latch swung to the right, freeing the lid. With both hands, she opened the chest.

"Why, this doesn't make any sense at all," Aubrey said in surprise.

"I'm sure it most certainly does. Tell me what you've found."

"There's only a small knife, a pocket knife…nothing different than one would buy at a sporting goods store. And there is nothing else to be seen. Are you sure you have brought us to the right place, Tara?"

"I can not explain until you have completed your task. Follow my instructions as I report them to you. Pick up the knife. Now, place it in your pocket. There you go. Now with both hands, slam shut the lid to the chest."

Aubrey peered, once more, into the depths of the chest. Still nothing, just an empty space. She slammed it down with all her might. The latch, of its own will, swung into place.

"As I said before, this unique chest holds all the powers you have. However, any given power will only be revealed to you when you need it. The contents of the chest will forever change. It has been waiting for you since you were born. And not all that you will discover in the chest is meant for pain. One item may be used to spread happiness, while another may be for the purpose of curing. For the wrath of Wild Edric, you will need only the knife. While its thrust may not be what kills him, it will be instrumental in the final outcome."

"But it is just a simple knife. Small enough to kill a squirrel, perhaps. Not to mention, if there were real danger, I would have to take the time to fumble it open first."

"Patience, please. Most things in the world of fair folk are not as they seem. Yes, it is a knife, at first glance. Stand here in front of me. Now hold the knife in your hand, closed as it is, and repeat these words:

Weapon of power
Strike evil that appears
With magic and faith
Release my fears."

Just as she had transformed in the garden, the first evening she met Tara, Aubrey became a beautiful fairy once again. The brilliant green dress was made of Laurel leaves. The shoes were a bit fancy, as was the opinion of Tara. Aubrey, however, loved the Lily of the Valley flowers that dangled around their tops. She felt for the headband. Her back tingled from the slight weight of the thin, translucent wings. Something new that she hadn't noticed before... a broach was buckled to one side of her dress. From it, hung a dagger in a sheath.

"May I," she asked Tara.

"Yes, of course."

Aubrey slowly pulled the dagger from its holder. How it sparkled and reflected the sun.

"Ah, you just found one of its powers."

"What do you mean?"

"Let its blade reflect the sun toward that mound over there. At the same time whisper the words fairy fire."

As sure as she did, the sun's rays lit the mound into a ball of fire. There was a soft crackling sound. Poof! It disappeared toward the sky in a ball of swirling smoke.

"That will take care and a very steady hand. Thankfully it will only happen at your wish and with your words."

"Can I defeat the Dark Elf with it?"

"That is yet to be seen. Your dagger holds much more. Come sit by me here on this log. Do not be worried about work. Time has not passed in the least."

Aubrey caught sight of Malvina far off down the path.

"Do not encourage her. Malvina is the very best listener of all fairies. Her job is to listen, translate, and report. She can hear us from there, and she will be satisfied with that."

"Who does she report to...Grandmom, Queen Mab?"

"Our concern right now is getting you ready for battle. Just to be safe let's get that dagger back into your pocket. Repeat after me:

Weapon of power
You've done your best
To save our worlds
On this quest."

Aubrey was once again in her work clothes. For a while Tara explained the other powers she could conjure with her knife. They traveled back to the garden above. As they parted, Aubrey could still see Malvina, waving gently from below. Aubrey looked at the time on her phone. No time had passed, just as Tara promised. She took the long way to the garden shop. As she turned down Third Street, she knew at 8:30 in the morning, Telford would be well into his first class at school. Maybe she would catch sight of his mother. No sign of anyone at 198 Third Street. She did, however, notice that the 'for sale' sign next door had been taken down. Nothing else seemed out of place. There was a woman sweeping the porch at the pewter shop. Aubrey's window was down, and they waved at each other.

"Hello there," bellowed the woman.

Aubrey turned toward the curb and pulled to a stop. "Hi," said Aubrey with her sweet smile. "I'm…"

"No need to introduce yourself. You just got back into town. Telford can't stop talking about his new friend Aubrey. You seem to be really good for him. He's got special qualities. Some qualities his school friends don't understand. I wouldn't call them friends anyway. And I heard you got a job over at Crabapple Corner."

"Yes, I did. I'm headed that way. It's my first day."

"Wouldn't seem like much to do this time of year."

"That is true, but I might be doing computer work, as well. I know it might seem early to mention this, but I would love to come back to your store and do some Christmas shopping for the inn."

"Anytime is fine. The season, of course begins as early as anyone wants it to. I'm Rachell, by the way."

"It's been very nice to meet you. I'll be back soon."

"Bye, now." She went back to her sweeping, and watched as Aubrey pulled off down the street. As soon as Aubrey was out of sight, she ran into the store. "Hey! Theodore, put down what you're doing and get out here!"

Theodore and Rachell Emerson owned Ye Olde Melting Pot on Third Street. An unlikely couple, as he was tall and thin with a quiet manner. She was short and stout. The perfectly square glasses were deliberately placed toward the end of her nose. They both wore black rubber boots, perhaps to save their everyday shoes from the results of melting and molding pewter.

"What is it, Rachell? What is all this fuss?"

"You'll never believe who just stopped in front of the store."

"Woman, you surely did not call me from my important work to play guessing games. Now just spill it!"

"Aubrey Bhaltair stopped to say a simple hello. Said she would be back to do some Christmas shopping. With the way things have been, we sure could use some of the Bhaltair money to get us through the first of the year. Now listen, husband. When she comes back put on your best customer service act. She may send her friends this way."

"I don't see why you're getting so worked up. Can't she just use her magic powers and conjure up some Christmas presents?"

"Now you hush. Those are rumors, and it's important that we treat her nicely for Telford's sake. He deserves a friend. According to his mom, and how he's always beaming, she's a real good fit. You don't believe in that fairy magic anyway. Now do you?"

"I suppose not, but you never know."

"Just don't go being rude next time she comes around."

"Alright woman."

He went back to his work, and with a smile on her face she returned to her sweeping. Times were hard for the Emersons since the big box stores came to town. People were more willing to pay just a small bit of change for something made in China. At Ye Olde Melting Pot every item was made right on site, crafted by the hands of Theodore and Rachell Emerson. It was considered an artisan's shop. Festivals and celebrations provided unique shopping experiences for tourists and the spending community of Ste. Germaine. The town's two most profitable times of the year were Jour de Fete in August and the Christmas Festival in December. Thank goodness they did not have a payroll to make.

Living above their shop helped with expenses, as well. Their building was listed on the historic register. At three stories, it was one of the tallest in the historic section of Ste. Germaine. The upper level provided Rachell with a nice view of some of the surrounding homes. She could see The Petit Jardin easily, but nothing interesting, she decided, ever happened there. Of late, she was mostly interested in the new neighbor that had moved in across the street. Theodore had no interest in her nosiness. His focus was on the worries of the business.

After sweeping inside and out, Rachell tended to the customer orders in a file on the counter. Opening the folder she found only three. They didn't amount to much, but she reported them to Theodore who said they would be completed by day's end. After that, he would focus on ornaments. The Christmas Festival would be here in a few months. Theodore had high hopes for the holidays and the purse it would bring.

Aubrey was looking forward to her first real day of work at Crabapple Corner. She parked in back of the storage shed and headed to the office. Both Martin and Betty were waiting for her with open arms. After hugs were shared, Aubrey put her purse away in the office. She put her phone in the back pocket of her jeans, and hung her sunglasses from the collar of her shirt.

"Here you go," said Betty. She pinned a nametag on Aubrey's shirt. It was hand printed, and similar to Betty and Martin's. "If you can figure out one of them programs on the computer, maybe you can print us up some fitting nametags."

Aubrey answered, "I don't see any cars or customers in the lot. Are you okay if that is the first job I do?"

"Certainly," answered Betty. "Martin, show Aubrey to the computer."

They went back to the outer office and Aubrey sat down in front of a brand new computer.

"Martin, this is a very nice set up."

"Maybe for someone who understands it. We used to do all of our billing by hand, much to the disagreement of our son,

Martin Jr. He bought us this about six months ago. He wasn't satisfied with the way we do the business end of things. Don't get me wrong. He means well and we're very proud of him. He earned a business degree from the university in Cape. But he vowed that he would not follow in his parent's footsteps. His kind heart got the best of him. So in his spare time he does our books. The right way I suppose. We're the shoebox operation you always see on one of them sitcoms. Like I said, he's a wonderful son and takes care of that side of things. So you have Martin Jr. to thank for that fancy silver computer."

"Martin, this computer even has Microsoft Word. That's what I can use to make our nametags. Do you want a particular font for our names?"

"Huh?"

"I mean do you want me to choose the lettering for our nametags?"

"Sure, just keep it simple."

"Martin, when we have some time, I can make you not so nervous around this computer. You'll be impressed with some of its features. And I'm sure your son would love that you tried."

"Hmmm."

"I'm not trying to push you, but you are a very young man. Being connected can help your business."

"Betty is waiting on me to help with the haystacks. People like to use them for their fall decorating. Why don't you surprise us with those nametags."

"Will do, Martin."

Aubrey felt at home working with computers. This one had everything she needed and was comfortable working with it. It took just a few minutes to create their nametags. She chose a font for Crabapple Corner similar to the one on the sign out front. Under Martin and Betty's names she had it read 'Owner'. She added 'Growing With You' to all of the badges. After the document was printed she found a pair of scissors. She was accustomed to this kind of work. At the Botanical Garden in St. Louis, her supervisors called upon her many talents and her jobs were endless. Oftentimes she would work at gardening, office duties, and customer service all in the same day. She enjoyed the technology aspect, but tending to flowers made her much happier. Nametags were cut and placed in the plastic jackets that Martin had left for her.

She went outside and could see that Martin and Betty were on the parking lot talking to a man next to a black Chevy Camaro. There were a lot of things that they had not discussed with her, including when to interrupt. She went back inside, placed their nametags on the desk, pinned hers on, and went for a walk around the grounds. She wanted to make a meaningful to-do list. Cleaning pots and sweeping didn't seem like enough work. Aubrey wanted to take this job seriously. And she had really hoped it would take her mind off (dare she say even in the secret places of her mind) being a half-fairy. She moved back to Ste. Germaine to relieve the stress of the hard-to-manage problems of St. Louis. Once she arrived, her problems seemed to multiply. How could that happen in such a small town? This was to be her escape. But from the moment she arrived brand new mysteries with unanswered questions seemed to be found beneath a tree, in a parlor, or in the earth below. No one would ever believe the changes that had taken place in her life. One thing was for sure. The gentry, to which she now felt a part of, made it very clear... she had responsibilities to fulfill and she had no choice in the matter.

"Hey, there she is," Betty called to her as she rounded the backside of the building.

Aubrey was shaken from her daydream. Betty, Martin, and the customer were right outside the office.

"Oh, sorry Betty. I finished the nametags. They're on your desk. I hope you don't mind, I found some scissors to do the cutting. Is there something you need me to do for...?"

"Aubrey this is Mike. Mike, Aubrey. Mike's here for a dozen bales of hay for a party he's throwin'. Here are the keys to the truck. Drive him around to the hay in back. Martin will be back there to load it up. Mike will give you an idea on where he lives.

You can follow him there. You think you can..."

"Oh, I wouldn't hear of it, Betty. I have plenty of guys on hand to unload it."

Aubrey answered, "I would love to help if it's needed."

"No worries," said Mike. "Aubrey, is it?"

"Yes. I just started working for Martin and Betty today."

"No kidding, I just started needing hay today." He smiled.

Martin and Betty laughed. Mike hopped into the cab, and Aubrey confidently drove the truck around to the hay at the edge of the property. Martin met them there and he and Mike loaded the bales onto the pickup.

"That should do it," Martin said when the last bale was loaded.

"We really appreciate the business, Mike."

"Don't mention it. Being new to town, it feels good knowing I have a go-to place for things I need around the outside of the house. I'll send Aubrey back in good fashion."

Martin nodded. "Aubrey you follow Mike. Let his guys unload the hay. On your way back, pick up some sandwiches for lunch from Annabelle's."

"Okay. See you and Betty in a bit."

Aubrey followed Mike north on Little Rock Road. A beautiful estate came into view. It was framed with a pristine white wooden fence. The entrance was made of two massive stone pillars that supported a doublewide security gate. It opened just as Mike turned off the main road. She followed his Camaro up a wide, blacktop drive, around a two-story farmhouse to the back. He motioned for Aubrey to back the truck up to an opening in a very large barn. She stayed in the truck.

"You have the option of getting out, you know." Mike startled her from the passenger side window.

"Ok, for a minute. Your guys will be done soon. Then I need to get those sandwiches and head back to the garden. It's my first day, and I'm trying to put my best foot forward."

"Well, the nametag is quite impressive. What else have you done?"

"When I was making the nametags this morning, I was able to check out their computer system. But like I said it's my first day. Martin and Betty are wonderful people. They're kind of giving me a loose reign on how I might help out the business. Without seeming rude, why are you so interested in what I do, what I'm doing for Martin and Betty?"

"Whoa there little filly. No worries from me. We're both new in town, aren't we? At least that's what Martin said. I just like to take the pulse of things. This is a small town, but it's big on critique. So, tell me about yourself."

"I just arrived to town less than a month ago. I'm hoping to start over here in Ste. Germaine. What about you?"

"I, too, would like a fresh start. Since arriving to town a few months ago I've become a regular customer of Crabapple Corner. They've given me a lot of tips on how to spruce up this old place. Martin said to make you feel welcome. I hope I've accomplished that."

Aubrey smiled. "What do you plan on doing with the hay, anyway?"

"I put together a big party to raise money for the Veterans of Missouri. It's planned for the weekend before Thanksgiving. We call it A Heroes Hoedown. There are hayrides, a bonfire, ghost stories, and a very expensive sit-down dinner... It's an evening of fun fall activities to benefit veterans."

"I've never known a veteran. It is admirable that you are raising awareness and helping them. Your hoedown sounds like a lot of fun. If you put together a flier, I'm sure Martin and Betty will let me put it in the window. If I can get a website up and running I could post it there, as well."

"That would be very helpful. I only know a few of the townspeople. If your website could reach some of the more affluent folks, I'd be grateful. Not many people are willing to pay a hundred dollars a plate for a meal, even if it is for a good cause."

"Drop off a flier at the garden shop, or even a mock up and I'll see how far I can take it. Looks like your men are finished. I better head back into town to pick up lunch. It was nice to meet you."

When Aubrey pulled away, she could see the farmhouse in her rearview mirror. It was made of large stone and painted white. There was a balcony that formed the roof of the front porch below. She wished she had paid better attention to the house when she had been closer. There may be another delivery of some kind, she thought, as the party gets closer. Surely he could never be the Dark Elf. Up until now, being on the lookout had slipped her mind. You just don't ask a man if he's a dark elf. She felt the gentry had not taught her enough. Is Grandmom taking things for granted? Does Tara want her to fall on her face, or do they all just think she needs to put her big girl pants on and learn this stuff on her own? She swerved to miss a dead opossum in the road. Her mind wandered to other things. Why was she picking up lunch so early? And her day ended at twelve. Surely she wouldn't get paid to eat and then leave. Her life in Ste. Germaine, Missouri, to be sure, was not a simple one. She honked once as she pulled the truck around the back of the building.

"I brought your sandwiches. One is turkey, the other ham. I wasn't sure so I thought you could choose or split and share."

"What kind did you get for yourself?"

"I didn't. It will be the end of my shift pretty soon. And I really wanted to feel like I did more today than make a few name tags."

"But Aubrey, you have. We've already gotten a phone call from Mike saying you are a breath of fresh air for this place, and you have excellent customer service skills."

"Wow, that's very nice. I'm glad, and it's only my first day. You two go ahead and eat. I'd like to sweep up the hay area so it's tidy for the next customer. Then I'm going to walk around a bit, and continue to make a to-do list for you to approve."

"Okay, Aubrey. If you insist."

Aubrey made quick work of the strewn-about hay. Then she pulled a pencil and folded piece of paper from her back pocket. It was easy to find things to place on the list. The first item she wrote was to paint the fence and the Crabapple Corner sign. The fence wasn't as nice as the one that surrounded Mike's estate, but a fresh coat of white paint would seem more welcoming to the customers. A car pulled into the lot and stopped just past the sign.

"You have any good pumpkins here?" a man yelled out his window.

"We sure do. Head on over to the gift shop area. There is a variety by the front door. I'll meet you there."

"I need three large ones and two small ones. They're for my front porch steps. Don't want to disappoint the trick-or-treaters, now do I?" The man laughed out loud.

"How about if you pick out the ones you like, and I'll write the prices down. That way we won't be moving them in and out of the store."

"Sounds like a plan."

He chose the five he wanted, while Aubrey wrote the prices down. As he loaded them into his trunk, she went inside to look for the register. Aubrey felt uneasy, both about the man, and finding that there was no register. Just then Martin appeared at the doorway.

"Hello, my name's Martin and this is Aubrey. Are you new to town?"

"Doesn't matter, just want to get the big ones carved for the trick-or-treaters."

"Of course."

Aubrey chimed in. "Would you like to look at our pattern books? There are lots of interesting designs that are popular with the kids. We have princesses, super heroes, and even cartoon characters."

"No, I won't be needing that. I have my own designs right up here. You know, the scary ones," he said tapping a finger on his forehead.

"Let's get you checked out then."

Martin nodded at her as she stared down at the check out counter. There was no register. It was a very simple accountant's adding machine with a roll of white paper. It was very old.

She could clearly see what Martin Jr. had meant. She punched in each price separately followed by the plus key. After the total appeared on the paper, she found a tax sheet next to the machine. The clear packing tape that held it in place was curling up at its four corners. She tallied the two.

"That will be twenty-five dollars and ninety cents."

He handed her thirty dollars and said, "Keep the change. Looks like you guys can use it. Kind of behind the times here."

With the pumpkins already in the trunk of his grey Ford Focus, he made a right out of the lot, and pulled away as quickly as he had arrived.

Aubrey spoke up, "Martin, I know not all of our customers will be as nice as Mike, but do we usually get some unfriendly ones, as well?"

"Aubrey, I want to make it very clear. We do not talk about a customer. We don't know that man or his lot in life. A friendly business, that's what I want to be known for."

"You are right, Martin. I'm sorry."

"It's time for you to head home. Tomorrow, we're going to talk more about how to check people out with their purchases. Betty loves this part of the job, but there may be times when she's unavailable. I know the adding machine may seem a bit out of date, but it works for us, and I'll show you how we take credit cards, as well."

"Absolutely. Hey Martin, can I devote thirty minutes each day to the website?"

"Of course you can."

"Great. I'm going to get my purse and say goodbye to Betty. See you tomorrow."

Aubrey took the same route home that she had traveled just a few hours earlier.

Third Street was two-way so she came at it from the other end. Telford wouldn't be home from school for a few more hours. She wanted meeting his mother to seem random, not forced. Secretly she hoped that Rachell Emerson would not be on the front porch of Ye Olde Melting Pot. No Rachell, no Telford's mother, no one. She did notice the porch next to Telford's house. There were large and small pumpkins lined up on the steps to the landing of the porch. Surely that was a coincidence. As she slowly passed the house she remembered Martin's customer service policy. We don't know this man, or his lot in life. This might not even be him. Nonetheless, Aubrey had an uneasy feeling. After all, Grandmom had told everyone in the gentry to be on the lookout. Who might the Dark Elf be?

"Have you eaten lunch?" Merle asked when she entered the kitchen. "I made quiche. There are strawberries, as well."

"Wonderful!" She sat down and ate while Merle tidied up the kitchen. "Is Grandmom home?" It just now occurred to her that her grandmother did not have a car.

"Remember, she is in a meeting with Queen Mab, and will be home just after dinner. She asked if you could write down your work schedule for her."

"I will. And, no, I didn't see anything or anyone suspicious."

"You don't seem absolutely sure. Was there something that didn't seem quite right or out of place?"

"There was a man who came into the garden shop. I found him a bit on the rude side. Martin encouraged me to give him the benefit of the doubt. On my way home I discovered he might be Telford's new neighbor."

"What stood out about him?" He took a pad and pencil from one of the kitchen drawers and placed it next to Aubrey's plate.

"I'm not sure. Like I said, I don't want to criticize a perfect stranger."

"You don't understand. The smallest detail might be the one that is our clue. Write down what you remember most about your encounter."

Aubrey pushed her plate aside and began to write: quick, rude, aloof, unexplainable, it doesn't matter, the scary ones, behind the times. She handed the paper to Merle. "I don't know if this amounts to anything," Aubrey said, "but here you go."

Merle read the items. "I'll keep it for this evening's meeting. If you think of anything else let me know. No detail is too small. And Aubrey, Grandmom will be very proud if you help defeat the Dark Elf."

Aubrey washed her dishes and put them away. "Merle, has anyone called to ask about the inn? It would be great to have it filled up for the holidays."

"No, nothing so far. I can see by the look on your face that you have a little scheme to decorate the inn in red and green."

"Don't forget the twinkling lights!" she said and went upstairs to the Flora Room. She pulled her work notes from her back pocket. Not much of a list, she thought. But a website and a few touches around the property of Crabapple Corner would bring in more customers. More customers meant more for her to do. She remembered what Merle said about Grandmom being proud of her. Was she proud that Aubrey had a job, graduated from college, or had money saved? Or was she waiting for Aubrey to have a nervous breakdown over all of this half-fairy, Dark Elf business? If she failed in helping to defeat the Dark Elf, would Grandmom send her back to St. Louis? Would it matter?

Aubrey went upstairs to sketch and take her mind off the meeting.

Grandmom entered the kitchen just as Ignatius popped out from behind the wood-burning stove. Grandmom nodded near the kitchen window, and Tara appeared. She began, "Now that we are all here, does anyone have anything to report? I know it has only been a short while, but this is the best way for us to begin. It gives a foundation. Aubrey, Merle tells me that you have something to contribute."

"Yes, Grandmom. I met a man at work today. He is new in town."

"Go on."

"He stopped by the shop to buy pumpkins. His manner was a bit rude and abrupt. When he was asked, he didn't want to tell much about himself. I don't know his name, but I'm pretty sure I do know where he lives."

"And where is that?"

"I believe he bought the house on Third Street, right next to Telford and his mother. When I drove by there on my way home I saw what looked like the exact pumpkins I had sold to him this morning."

"That is something worth noting. Please keep me posted. Try to make a friend of him if he comes to your shop again."

"I will, Grandmom."

"Please everyone, have a seat and get comfortable. I have much to tell."

Aubrey and Merle sat at the table, while Ignatius, as Brownies do, sat next to the stove with his knees pulled tightly to his chest. Tara perched herself atop a cabinet.

"Now, then," Grandmom began, "as you know I met with Queen Mab today. She had very useful information to share. As I have stated before, Wild Edric has powers, powers of a sorcerer. He does have weaknesses, but we must find them out. At present he is recovering from his journey. While we do not know who he is, we do know he is weak. This does us no good. Day-by-day he gains his strength. The Queen and I suspect he will keep his identity hidden during his recovery. This could take months, for no Dark Elf would dare to fight a battle unless he thought he could win. We, on the other hand, know full well that we will win. The gift of time has been granted. We must take advantage of it. Queen Mab knows that you will be fighting both as individuals and as an army of four."

Merle interrupted, "That means…"

Grandmom continued, "Yes, that means that I am here for guidance. I am under the orders of The Queen to keep myself out of harm's way. If something were to happen to her, I must step in and take her place. I have known this for a great many years. If my visions are true, Queen Mab will never die. I am comfortable being second in command. It is this way for a reason. If it changed, so then would my relationship with this gentry. That is not my wish. Here are four envelopes, each with your name on them. Go off by yourselves. Do not share the contents with anyone, not even each other. Inside, there is one word or phrase. Study this. Ask yourself the following: What does it mean to me and how can it help me defeat Edric? But first, you must remember to keep it a secret. Find out everything you can."

Tara spoke up from atop the cabinet. For the first time Aubrey could see a sparkle to her wings. It was amber gold to match the trunk of the Elder tree. Her cheeks were rosy and she had a tiny pointed nose. She didn't look so tough, there, under the brightness of the kitchen light. "Grandmom, how much time do you think we have?"

"Tara, it is good to be thinking these things. Queen Mab and I believe that the winter will come and go. Dark Elves, even at their strongest, do not like the colder weather. Even though we have forecasted springtime for the mayhem to begin, always, always be on guard. Be alert and discuss findings among yourselves. Every day must be a day of preparation. And do not trust anyone outside of our gentry." She looked at Aubrey and then continued, "Aubrey, you have a sweet and gentle nature. And yes, Telford is a dear young friend. In a short time, you will think sweetly of Betty and Martin, as well. But do not," and she raised her voice, "do not share anything with them. Not even the slightest bit of your half-fairy side. Also, I know without doubt that the Emersons have their eyes on us. We cannot afford for the gentry to weaken at the hands and words of outsiders. The four of you have been patient. Are there any more questions?" She looked at each one in turn.

"I have a suggestion, if I may," said Ignatius. "I will keep the fire burning low in the stove through the night. Perhaps we should each study the contents of our envelopes, then burn them one-by-one in the stove. I will guard it, of course, until the last ember has turned to ash."

Grandmom spoke, "That is an excellent idea. You are thinking like a true member of the gentry, as always. Anything else? Very well then, let us retire."

"Grandmom," stammered Aubrey. The room became silent.

"Yes, please continue."

"Don't be upset with me for asking this, but I believe she is a member of the gentry. Does Malvina have a part in all of this? Does she have a say?"

"No question would cause me to be angry, dear Aubrey. You are thinking. This is what's important. However, Malvina's part in this is very subtle, and will be revealed when Edric is conquered. While she is very comfortable in this world, she must be treated like a princess. There is much more to tell about sweet, lovely Malvina. I will save that for another time."

"Grandmom, could it be possible to take Wild Edric to our underworld, where our number would be greater than four?"

"Aubrey, I am very proud of you. These are things to consider and to share with the gentry. Never forget that all of you, including Malvina, mean everything to me. The evening is late. May tomorrow's sun shine down upon you all. To bed we must go."

Before going upstairs, Ignatius showed Aubrey how to turn the handle on the wood-burning stove. "I'll be here," he said, "if you need any help."

"Thanks, Ignatius. Hopefully I won't disturb you."

The gentry dispersed. Aubrey wondered if Tara was lonely out in the garden, with only the trees to keep her company. She would make it a point to say hello to her on her way out tomorrow.

Upstairs, Aubrey looked about her room. It was still a bit drab. She didn't own any personal pictures to display. Nothing in the room was hers except the fairy snow globe. What a wonderful gift it was, and from such a sweet young man...a friend. She went over to the globe and gave it a gentle shake. The glitter went to the top, then slowly fell in a million mirrored pieces to the base. The fairy in the globe reminded her of Malvina. Perhaps because she was all alone by a tree. Could it be that Tara and Malvina were related? Why was Malvina next to a tree when she first saw her? She returned the globe to her nightstand, then took off her necklace. Could Tara guard the whole house from the tree? Aubrey realized she was far too worried about everything. She needed a nice hot shower. Afterwards, she laid out a fresh pair of jeans and a cozy sweatshirt for tomorrow. The envelope was still in the front pocket of the jeans in the corner of her bathroom. She took it out and tossed the jeans into the hamper. Carefully she opened it and pulled out a small piece of paper from inside. It was folded in half. Breathe in, breathe out. The word Hawthorn was hidden within the fold, in a pen she did not recognize. She whispered it three times, then crumpled up both the note and the envelope. She hurried off down the stairs to the kitchen.

Ignatius was curled up and fast asleep behind the stove. He stirred as Aubrey managed the small door open. She would never forget, or share her word. The paper caught fire against a small chunk of glowing wood. After a while Aubrey closed the door, sure the piece of paper and the word were gone forever. Ignatius smiled to himself as she walked back upstairs.

Tara came into the kitchen by way of the cracked window, and Merle waited until the coast was clear just after midnight. The only gentry member left was Ignatius.

He loved this gentry so. It was his family. Most days he forgot that each was a member of the magical folk society. Grandmom was the overbearing mother that meant well. Merle was like a father, and Aubrey was a brand new friend. Tara was the sister that anyone would be lucky to have. She was brave and true. As he stirred the largest of the few glowing coals, the last of the secret words was tossed in. Ignatius stood back and wafted the smoke toward him. "Ah," he said out loud. "Let the folly begin."

Part Three

OCTOBER 29

Aubrey was sorting Halloween candy into bowls when the doorbell rang. It was Telford. "Hey you," she said, " you know you don't have to ring the bell. Are you home from school already?"

"Yep, and I'm off until Monday. The teacher's have a workday tomorrow. Then they have parent teacher conferences tomorrow night. That means everyone gets off on Friday."

"Friday's Halloween. I know you said you weren't dressing up, so if it's okay with your mom you can help me hand out candy."

"If you still want to meet her, she's home right now for a little while until she goes to work. I can leave my bike here, and we can walk."

"Where does your mom work, Telford?"

"She works at the tack shop."

"What's that?"

"Oh, a place for horse people to shop. I mean they sell saddles, feed, and lots of other stuff. They also give horse-riding lessons. My mom has loved horses all of her life. She owned one when she was little, but had to give it away when her parents died in a house fire."

"Oh, Telford, I am so sorry."

"That's okay. It was before I was born. She got out okay because a neighbor helped her. She was seventeen then and on her own, so there was no way to keep her horse. She's been working at the tack shop ever since. Luckily, she gets to give some of the riding lessons."

90

"Telford, I hope it's okay if I ask this, but where is your dad?"

"Sure, it's okay. He died, too. I'm not sure how, but mom said he was a very mean man and the only thing he ever did right was have a boy like me. I didn't know him, so there's not much to miss. It would be okay to have a dad, I guess."

They made their way to Third Street in no time.

"Have you met your new neighbor?"

"I waved to him once. He didn't say anything. Mom said to stay out of his business and he'll stay out of ours. I wish Mom had more friends. I'm glad you're going to meet her."

"Me, too."

As they walked closer to the house the screen door to 198 Third Street opened. There stood a beautiful young woman with long flowing black hair. It was pulled back in a red and white ribbon. She wore a starched light blue denim shirt tucked into skintight jeans. Black boots with silver studs clicked on the porch as she came out to hold the door open. She reached out her hand. "Hi, I'm Telford's mom, Laura. Sorry I haven't been available until now to meet you."

They all went in and sat down in the living room. It was decorated in light blues and tans. Over the fireplace hung a picture of a magnificent palomino horse.

"That's okay. I've been pretty busy myself. I hope it's okay that Telford hangs around at the inn sometimes."

"I'm grateful that he does. I guess you know I work a lot of hours at the tack shop. He promises he's getting his homework done."

"I ask him that as well. Also, if it's after dark either Merle or I walk him home."

"Mrs. Emerson said you drove by a few times."

"I did, but I didn't want to bother you by ringing the bell."

"Anytime that I'm home you're welcome to stop by."

"Laura, I was wondering if... Telford tells me you're working Halloween evening. And he insists that he's too old to dress up in a costume. Would it be okay if he helped me hand out candy?"

"I didn't think Grandmom believed in Halloween."

"You may be right about that. But I do have her convinced that it would be good for business if we have a more friendly, open door policy. Business shouldn't be as slow as it is."

"You're right. This is one of my favorite times of the year. For some reason fall leaves make people want to horseback ride."

"I'm not sure I know what you mean."

"People want to go horseback riding down a nice leaf covered trail. That's where I come in. They pay us to lead them. Best job in the world. And at Christmas, lots of the more well off families will give riding lessons as a gift. Being around the horses is way better than selling a pair of boots. Don't get me wrong. All aspects of the business are important, and the people I work for are very generous to me. Sorry to rush, but I've got to get there. I've never been late or taken off sick."

"It was very nice to finally meet you."

"You too. Telford, where's your bike?"

"It's back at the inn. We walked here."

They went outside and said their goodbyes. Laura got into an old Volkswagen Beetle.

"I love your car!"

"Thanks. I keep my truck at the shop."

Laura pulled away and Telford and Aubrey headed back to the inn. Aubrey looked back over her shoulder and saw a man peering out the window in the house next to Telford's. The old tattered curtain quickly closed.

When they reached the inn, Telford gave Aubrey a hug. "I can't wait until Halloween," he said.

"Me, too. Come early. I have a few more decorations to put out on the porch. How many trick-or-treaters do you think we'll have?"

"Even though people aren't used to the lights being on at the inn, the rest of the block is pretty busy. All of the businesses along your street give out candy. I'd say we might have maybe fifty kids. But don't worry about any left over candy!"

OCTOBER 30

Feeling blessed to have her job at Crabapple Corner; Aubrey wanted to be helpful and offered to work the Friday before Halloween. Also, Martin and Betty increased Aubrey's hours until one o'clock. The extra time was meant to work on the website. However, they still insisted that she stop for lunch, and get paid for that time, as well.

"Martin, I think you'll be pleased with what I've done with the website so far."

"Oh, we are. Martin Jr. keeps his eye on it and says you're doing a very good job. What's all this talk about sponsors? I didn't quite understand what he was going on about."

"I made a few phone calls last week, and was able to persuade two of our suppliers to take out an ad on our website. They pay us to be on our page, and we make money."

"You really are going to fix things up around here, aren't you? And I've had at least three customers comment on the fence."

"I'm glad to do it. I've never had a job that I've loved so much."

Betty walked into the office. "Have either of you heard from the tree farm yet?"

They hadn't.

"Aubrey can you make a note of it? If they don't call by next Friday, give them a holler. Around mid November, they drop off seventy-five trees, some wreaths, and roping for the holiday sales."

"I'll take care of it," Aubrey said. "Also, are there any decorations for me to put up around the nursery?"

"There sure are. I'll show you where we keep them. Let's decorate a day or two before the tree delivery. I don't like to jump the gun like some of them big box stores."

"What about things for the gift shop? Do we normally have holiday items to sell, other than the trees?"

Martin spoke up. "That shipment is coming on Monday. I'll show you how to price things, and how to move things around in the shop. There are also some items from last year in the supply room."

One o'clock came quickly and Aubrey headed for her car. Mike pulled up and got her attention.

"Hey, I just wanted to thank you for posting my event on your website. I'm certain it helped. All dinner spots have been reserved."

"No, problem. Martin and Betty insisted that I do it on company time. They really like having you as a customer. One thing you could do as a small thank you..."

"Sure, anything."

"Are you on Facebook?"

"From time to time."

"If you could go to our Facebook page, like it, and share it. Talking it up would really help out our business. It also leads people back to our website."

"That seems easy enough."

"Thanks," Aubrey said, and began to get into her car.

"Hey, not so fast. I was wondering if you might be available to be my plus one at the Veteran's celebration."

"That's very nice, but I couldn't afford it. Surely you know someone else."

"Even if I did, I'm asking you. And you've misunderstood. I'd like you to be my date. Under no circumstances are you to pay. I've botched things up, haven't I?"

"No, of course not."

"If you'd like some time to think it over..."

"No, it's not that. What's the attire?"

"I think you look great just as you are, but I understand that women like to know what other women are wearing. Am I right?"

Aubrey picked some hay off the front of her sweatshirt, and smiled.

"I suppose it's meant to be semi-formal. At my previous

fundraisers, many of the wives wore casual dresses, and the men khakis. Everyone has the option to change for the hay rides and bonfire that take place later in the evening."

"What are you going to wear?"

"For dinner, I'll be wearing a black suit with a white shirt. I've been told that it makes me look dashing."

"This has me very nervous, but I'm leaning toward saying yes."

"Come on. It will be lots of fun. Remember I'm just as nervous as you are. Save for a few of my old friends there, most of the guests are townspeople. You will be my comfort zone."

"Alright, I'll go."

"That's outstanding! I'll send a car for you at 4:30. Cocktails at 5, and dinner at 6. Remember to bring comfy clothes for later. And don't worry, you won't need to bring your own hay. I promise you'll have fun."

OCTOBER 31

"Thanks for inviting me. My mom was really glad I had something to do tonight. She doesn't like me staying home by myself. And she thought I might be afraid tonight... because it's Halloween."

"I'm glad you're here, too. Grandmom said she had an appointment, and Merle is working in the greenhouse."

"Have you been inside the greenhouse yet?"

"No, but we have one at Crabapple Corner. I'm sure they're all pretty much the same. There are lights that help the plants grow. Some greenhouses have a watering system."

Trick-or-treaters came and went. Aubrey and Telford made each one tell a joke before choosing from the candy bowl. Telford had been right; there were about fifty in all.

"Merle said we are going to have two woman staying here for a few days. He called it a girl's get-away. So I'm going to take the Halloween decorations down tomorrow. If you'd rather ride your bike or play with a friend I'd understand, or... you can help. Fall decorations will be so much more inviting, I feel."

"Sure, I'll help."

"Perfect! If you get here early enough, there might even be some of Merle's pancakes."

"Wow, that sounds great. I know Mom is doing something with horses tomorrow. She said some new rich guy has a stable. Two horses are going to be delivered. She's good with horses, you know."

"I could tell she has a soft spot for them."

"I really hope she has one of her own someday."

"You're a very good son, Telford. Time to get you home."

Aubrey parked in front of his house. The house next door was dark, except for a small window on the side. It looked like a basement light. The pumpkins were glowing on the steps. The mystery man delivered in the scary department. Aubrey could make out a ghost and a witch. The third larger pumpkin looked more like a devil face.

Telford saw the pumpkins, as well. "Look. The new neighbor sure can carve a pumpkin."

"I noticed that. I'm going to walk you to the door, and have you turn on a few lights. Do you have a land line in the house?"

"Yep. Why?"

"You have my cell phone. If you need anything call me right away. I keep my phone on all of the time. If for some reason I don't answer, call the inn. Merle will most certainly answer."

"Thanks, but I'll be fine. The tack shop closes at nine thirty."

"I know, but just in case."

"Mom says I might get a cell phone for Christmas. Then we can text each other."

"I should probably get her number."

"I'm sure she'd be okay with that."

After Aubrey walked through a few rooms, Telford spoke up, "Time for me to watch some spooky movies on TV until Mom gets home. Thanks again for tonight."

"You're welcome. Don't stay up too late. Remember,

you're helping out tomorrow."

The tack shop wasn't too far from Crabapple Corner. The OPEN sign was still flashing. Aubrey went inside.

"Hi Laura."

"Hi, what a surprise. Everything ok with Telford?"

"Everything is fine. That's why I stopped in. I thought maybe we could exchange cell numbers. That way I could keep you posted on things like when he gets home safe. Or maybe you might need me to keep an eye on him, if you get called to work at the last minute."

"That's a great idea. Here's one of my cards. He stays by himself quite a bit, but it has been a comfort knowing he's with such a nice person who's looking out for him. He could have given you my number, but it was nice of you to stop in."

"No problem at all. He said he wanted to help with the fall decorations tomorrow. Would it be all right with you if I gave him a few dollars for helping out? My grandmother let me pretend I was an employee when I was little. I loved it when I got paid."

"I guess that would be ok. You're going above and beyond." Laura pulled the chain on the OPEN sign.

"Not really. Having Telford as a friend has been a real blessing. Have a safe drive home."

"You too."

The inn was dark when she arrived home. She walked around the house to the back door. Merle came out of the greenhouse and locked the door behind him.

"Not yet, Aubrey… in time," he said.

"That's ok Merle. I trust you. Oh, before I forget, Telford might come early enough for breakfast tomorrow morning. What are the chances you might make your blueberry pancakes?"

"Very good, I suppose."

Merle waited for Aubrey to lock the door to the inn behind her before going to the back house. Aubrey wondered why Merle didn't stay in one of the nicer rooms inside the inn. It was never at capacity. She turned her thoughts to the women coming for the girl's get-away. Merle would be able to tell her which room they were going to be in. She and Telford would give it some extra care.

After her shower, she settled into bed with her garden book. The bookmark was at page 156...The Hawthorn tree. These are not the type of facts, she thought, that would help in a time of emergency. What she really meant was a time of battle. Knowing how deep to plant a Hawthorn is not going to defeat Wild Edric the Dark Elf. Maybe Betty and Martin had some tree books at the nursery, or Telford might like to visit the library after their chores tomorrow. Surely there must be something special about a Hawthorn tree. Maybe the paper didn't mean a tree at all. Maybe it meant Nathanial Hawthorne, the American author. No, that name had a different spelling. He was, however, born in Salem, Massachusetts; a town known for its witches. It was time for sleep. She leaned to turn off the small lamp on her nightstand and noticed that the globe was not as it should be. It was facing the window to the right of the bed.

NOVEMBER 1

Telford walked to the inn. After pancakes, he and Aubrey made quick work of things.

"We are all finished with the downstairs and the front porch. Merle said the new guests will be staying in the Dahlia Room. So we are going to spend a little time sprucing it up."

"I've noticed that Mr. Merle doesn't climb the steps very much. Why didn't he put the guests in a room downstairs?" Telford asked.

"That is true. He isn't as young as he used to be. I enjoy helping out, and it makes me feel like I'm earning my keep."

"What does that mean... earning your keep?"

"I have a job and I get paid twice a month. But, Grandmom and Merle insist that I not pay rent, or even help with the grocery bills. So I feel like I'm contributing by doing the dishes, painting things, and cleaning the rooms. That is, when Merle lets me. He is very proud."

"I get it. It's like when my mom gives me an allowance for taking out the trash, and stuff like that."

"It is just like that. How do you feel about dusting while I change the bed linens and wipe down the bathroom?"

"That's a real easy job."

They headed downstairs to look for Merle. He was in the kitchen and had everything ready on the kitchen table; cleaning supplies, bedclothes, and towels for the bathroom.

"Thanks, Merle."

"No problem at all. Having you two doing all this work is like having responsible employees... like a regular business. If word gets out that we run such a tidy inn people might start coming. I'd love to have the inn busy and full of life... especially during the holidays. Here, I thought this might be a nice touch. I've been tending to these in the greenhouse."

"What are they?" asked Telford.

"I recognize those," answered Aubrey, "they're Dahlias."

"Hey, that matches the name of the room," Telford chimed in.

"Merle, these are perfect."

The Dahlia Room was located at the end of the hall, to the left, on the second floor. Merle thought they might like the option of using the reading lounge across from Aubrey's room. Aubrey and Telford worked for an hour or so. Aubrey imagined Mrs. Emerson taking note of the guests from the top floor window of her pewter shop. New life at the inn meant more to talk about.

"We did a great job, Telford. Your help is really appreciated around here. How would you feel about earning a few dollars for your hard work?"

"Taking money for doing small stuff like this wouldn't seem right. Besides, I mostly just like hanging around."

"I know, but Merle and I have decided that the inn might be getting busier soon, and we could really use your help with all the small chores. It would make both of our jobs easier. How does five dollars an hour sound?"

"Wow, do you mean it? I'll have to ask my mom!"

"You're mom and I have already talked about it, and she said yes. Plus, we have each other's numbers now, so she knows when you're with me, hanging out, working, or anything else."

"Okay, boss. What's next?"

"Well I'm afraid we are now officially off the clock. What would you say about going to the library? Don't worry, I know it's your day off from learning, but I'd really like us go. Then lunch at Annabelle's after. How does that sound?"

"Don't be surprised, but I kind of like the library. They have updated computers and a cool section for kids. Plus you'll need me to show you around. I'm sure a lot has changed since you were last in town."

"You're probably right. I do remember it being a bit of a distance, so let's take the car."

"First, can we go by my house so I can get my library card?"

"You don't carry a wallet?"

"No, I guess I've never really needed to."

"Well, now is a good time to start. You'll need something to put your money in when we go Christmas shopping for your mom. Your first payday is today. I'll hold on to your money until we get you a wallet. You can also put your library card in it. Let's go to the mall after lunch. When is your birthday?"

"January twenty-fifth. I'll be twelve."

"We don't want to wait until then. Let's make it an early Christmas present."

"What if the kids at school make fun of me? I don't think any of the other boys my age have one."

"Then you'll just carry yours when you are with a more mature crowd."

"You're really nice, you know that, Aubrey?"

"Takes one to know one. Now let's go get your card."

They drove over to Third Street. It was a quiet Saturday. While most of the houses were decorated for Halloween, the house next door looked vacant once again. No sign of the pumpkins. Mrs. Emerson conveniently appeared on the porch of the pewter shop.

Telford spoke first. "Hi, Mrs. Emerson. Do you know my friend, Aubrey?"

"I do. We met the other day. What kind of mischief are the two of you up to on this nice Saturday?"

Telford continued, "We're just stopping by the house to get my library card. Hey, Aubrey. You didn't tell me what you're going to look for at the library."

She remembered the tone in Grandmom's voice, 'Do not share the contents with anyone, not even each other.' There was no wavering from the severity of Grandmom's wishes.

"I like to read books about gardening. It was part of my major in college. When spring arrives I have big plans to help Merle get the garden area back in shape. We could use your help with that, Telford."

This took his mind off the library for a little while. He was excited about earning money. His mom worked very hard at the tack shop, and he had never been able to buy her anything. He vowed to himself right then and there that he would become an expert handyman who could save money in a brand new wallet. Who cares, he thought, about those bullies at school. No one he knew had a best friend like Aubrey. No one.

"Will there be any digging involved?" he asked, giving Aubrey a wink.

Mrs. Emerson cleared her throat. "You two are quite a pair."

Telford headed inside to get his card.

Mrs. Emerson went on, "I hear you have a date coming up. Being just back in town, you're not doing so bad for yourself."

"What do you mean, Mrs. Emerson?"

"First off call me Rachell. Word around town is you've been invited to a nice party at the new guy's big estate. Seems he has a lot to offer a small town girl like you. Sound about right?"

"I am attending a party. But I don't understand why it's

made the Ste. Germaine social word circles." Aubrey's response flustered Mrs. Emerson, and it showed.

"Well… well… what I meant was …"

Telford came out and locked the door behind him.

Aubrey interrupted Mrs. Emerson, "Have a great Saturday. C'mon Telford time for you to give me a tour of our little library. This small town girl is looking forward to reading some of those big books. It was nice to see you Mrs. Emerson."

And off they went, leaving Rachell Emerson to the emptiness of her front porch, feeling insulted.

"You're going to love the library. I can help you look for things. The kids at school don't know it, but the library can be kind of fun. They're pretty mean sometimes."

"That makes me very sad. But, if it helps, when I was little, kids at school made fun of me when my mom died. They said she deserved it. They thought I was different, and weren't afraid to tell me."

"Was it because of the bones buried in the garden?"

"Telford, my life is quite a mystery, I'll admit, but I'm certain there are no bones buried in the garden."

"If you say so. Can I use my shovel to help with spring planting, anyway?"

"Now that sounds more like it."

Telford was proud to give Aubrey a tour of the library. He showed her all of the sections he thought she would like to use- adult fiction, biography, gardening, and the reference room.

"Will you be okay while I play games on one of the computers?"

"That'll work out great. I'll come by in a little bit. Otherwise, if you need me, I think I'll be in the gardening section or maybe the reference."

Telford said, "Why don't you get a library card first? You said you might like to check something out."

"That is a very good idea."

That was more easily said than done.

"Ma'am you will need proof of residency in the town of

Ste. Germaine."

"But I do live here."

"Then you should be able to prove it. We will accept a utility bill with your name on it."

"But I've only moved back to town a month or so ago. And I don't pay the bills at…" Aubrey stopped, realizing that she lived at home and had no real responsibilities except for her job. No wonder the likes of Rachell Emerson was all about the rumors of the new girl in town. How embarrassing, she thought. Feeling proud, and a bit upset, she decided to set things straight. Aubrey continued, "I'm sorry. Your job must require you to look at checklists and follow certain rules. My abruptness was unnecessary. However, I would like to have a library card. Would it help to know that Nola Bhaltair is my grandmother?"

"My apologies. I'm sure there is something I can do."

"I don't want you to make any exceptions for me. I just want to be able to check out books. Rest assured, permanent residency is in my future. I may be doing things out of order, that's all."

Just then Telford appeared at her side.

She continued, "And what better reference than Telford Chasseur. Am I right?"

Embarrassed by the last few minutes, the lady behind the computer said, "You, Miss Bhaltair, in just a moment, will be the newest cardholding member of the Ste. Germaine Library."

Aubrey glanced down at her nametag. It read Jenny Landon. "Jenny, my friend Telford and I have other errands to run today. When I come back, and if you're not here, will I be able to check out a book?"

"Of course, Miss Bhaltair. I'm printing out a card for you right now."

Aubrey and Telford headed back toward home.

"What are we doing now?" he asked.

"Let's come back to the library another time. I promised you a wallet, and a wallet you will have. We'll go to the mall in Cape Girardeau. Hang on a minute, I just want to text your mom and let her know. Then let's get some lunch from Annabelle's for our drive."

While waiting for their sandwiches, Telford played the video game in the corner of the diner. Aubrey's phone buzzed. There were two texts. One was a 'yes' response from Telford's mom. The second was from Mike. He sent a picture of a beautifully designed orchid tie with pastels of fuchsia and pink woven in and out of the pattern. She recognized the style to be Jerry Garcia. The message attached read, "Just in case this helps you pick out a dress."

A very thoughtful gesture, she thought, and reminiscent of something a prom date might do. She texted back, 'It does, thanks. What a great tie.' Send.

Her thoughts were interrupted by Telford's voice, "I think the sandwiches are ready."

"Ok, thanks." She picked up the sandwiches and paid for them at the counter.

"Maybe one day I'll be able to buy lunch."

"We'll see. Right now, you're focusing on saving for Christmas."

"Did my mom say it was okay?"

"She did. To Cape Girardeau we go. How do you feel about Christmas carols in November? I know of two radio stations that have already started playing them."

"We might as well. The mall will be decorated. If you can't beat 'em, join 'em."

They walked through most of West Park Mall. Aubrey saw a few dresses with potential in some of the shop windows. She made a mental note to look on line when she got home. In the meantime, she wanted the wallet to come from one of the department stores. They found the perfect one at JC Penney. It was a Relic brand wallet, dark chocolate brown, with tan stitching. She could tell that Telford was feeling a sense of pride. He asked the lady at the checkout if he could begin carrying it right then. She and Aubrey smiled at each other.

Walking back through the mall, Aubrey said, "Let's have a

seat here on this bench."

"Sure. Plus I want to take another look at my wallet. My mom is really going to like it. The color and stitching remind me of a saddle that she keeps in our garage. I like how it has the fun compartments on the inside." He took his library card out of his other pocket and slid it into one of the layered openings. "What's this clear one for?"

"That's for the driver's license you'll be getting in a few years."

"I promise to keep this wallet forever. It's one of the best gifts I've ever gotten." He began to put it back into his pants pocket.

"Not so fast, partner. Remember, today is pay day." Aubrey reached into her purse and pulled out two five-dollar bills. "Let me show you how to properly have money in your wallet. "The presidents should all face all the same way and right side up. Smaller bills go in front of the larger bills. You'll get the feel of which direction works for you, which back pocket, and so on. Always put it in the same place at home. I wouldn't take it to school unless there's an occasion when you think you might need it. One last thing... a wallet isn't meant to be a bank. Just keep a few dollars in it unless you're going shopping for a special occasion like Christmas. Otherwise, find a safe spot at home to keep the rest."

"I have a small box in my desk. I call it my treasure box. There are a few special things from my great grandpa."

"That's a perfect spot."

"Thanks, Aubrey. This is going to be the best Christmas ever. I can just tell."

"I couldn't agree more. Say, Telford, do you and your mom have big Thanksgiving plans?"

"I'm not sure. Luckily, the tack shop is closed."

"Do you remember what you did last year?"

"Yeah, I do. She cooked a nice meal just for the two of us."

"What would you think about coming to the inn for Thanksgiving? I'm not sure if we will have any guests, but Merle said he's making a turkey and all the trimmings. I can ask your mom, or you can."

"She doesn't work late tonight. I'll ask her then. Right after she sees my new wallet."

Telford threw his arms around Aubrey's neck. They sang Christmas songs all the way home. If they didn't know the words, they made up their own. She dropped Telford off at his house, and watched him get safely inside.

Back at the inn she saw a Jeep in the side lot. Must be the get-away girls, she thought.

"Here she is. Aubrey, this is Lisa and Kristi. They are here from Tennessee, and will be staying in the Dahlia Room."

Lisa spoke up, "We've seen it and it is so delightful. Merle said we have you to thank for doing the extra special touches. Fresh flowers and everything."

"You're welcome and we hope you'll enjoy your stay. There are some pamphlets in the hall near the front door. And the Visitor's Center is just two blocks down. Right now there is a demonstration of candle dipping. The live activities change most every day. Everything in the historic district is within walking distance. If you're thinking about chain stores and franchise restaurants, then you'll need to hop in your car. But the drive is very short."

Kristi responded, "Thanks for the information. We're going to have dinner out, then return. Merle said he would start a fire for us in one of the parlors."

"See you later on then," Aubrey said as they made their way down the front steps. "Merle, do they seem to get along? Are they normal?"

"Why do you ask?"

"I just don't think I have the stomach for another mysterious homicide…I mean suicide here at the inn."

"You're over thinking things, Aubrey."

"We must agree to disagree." With that, she headed upstairs to do some on-line shopping. Not wanting to go back to Cape, she was sure she could have something delivered in time for the party.

There was a brocade settee of blue and gold in the corner of her bedroom. From the window, she could see Tara in the Pine tree. Tara waved and smiled, as if seeing an old friend. Aubrey could tell she wasn't exactly looking her way. Suddenly, it dawned on her. Tara was the one that moved the snow globe to face her direction. While Aubrey was not upset by this, she did vow to talk with Tara. Could her magic move the globe, or did she have to enter Aubrey's room? As she began to put the globe back into its proper place, she changed her mind. The rambunctious fairy in the tree has only the gentry. She left the globe facing the garden. Tara continued to smile...now looking directly at Aubrey.

She recalled a few of the store names as she scanned the West Park Mall registry on her laptop. She remembered Charlotte Russe, Buckle, and Francesca's. There was a dress she had seen in one of the store windows. She just couldn't remember which one. After checking out the websites of all three, she found it to be a classic example of Goldilocks. The dresses at Charlotte Russe were much too casual, most being made of cotton. The dresses at Buckle were made of crushed velvet and satin materials. They were too fancy for a dinner in a barn. Finally, she found the dress she had remembered seeing in the window of Francesca's Boutique. It was a deep fuchsia with black lace at the waist. It hit just enough above the knees and had a peek-a-boo cut out back. The perfect amount of fancy. It suited her simple style of dressing. She wouldn't have to change at all for the bonfire and hayride. At dinner she would wear her black heels. As the evening progressed she would change into her black cowboy boots, and have her blue jean jacket for the cooler outside air. Add to cart, express shipping, order complete. One outfit, two looks... genius. Now to pick out the jewelry. She knew from experience that she spent too much time trying to choose the right jewelry for any special occasion. Getting it out of the way now would save her from panic when the evening arrived. Did she want to impress Mike? She wasn't sure.

She heard Merle call to her from the bottom of the stairs.

"Aubrey, I've started a fire in the parlor for our guests. There's a pot of chili on the stove. Would you like a bowl?"

"Sounds great, Merle. I'll be right down."

On her dresser she laid three pairs of earrings and two necklaces. She wondered about her hourglass and her knife. Being a fairy with secrets sure had its drawbacks. The hourglass necklace would seem arbitrary with her dress. After a while she chose a sensible, matching handbag. Her solution was to carry the necklace and knife in her black clutch, vowing to never let it out of her sight.

"I really am coming, Merle," she said placing the handbag by the jewelry.

Aubrey met Merle in the kitchen. "This smells delicious. Are you sure I should be eating in the parlor? I don't want to be in the way when Lisa and Kristi return.

"They're eating dinner in town. You should be fine."

She wished there had been time to find a book at the library on the Hawthorn tree. But checking it out would mean leaving a trail. On her next visit she would take supplies to make notes from any books she might find. How lovely it would be to read by the inn's fire. Next time, she thought. A good old-fashioned romance would make a fine read in the inn's beautiful parlor. Romance... she thought of Mike's beautiful Jerry Garcia tie. Would he be in the car that picked her up at the inn? Would there be nosey townspeople waiting to pass judgment on Nola Bhaltair's granddaughter? She snapped out of it and picked up the Southern Living magazine from the coffee table.

She wondered if other members of the gentry were further along in their quest for a strike against the Dark Elf. Was anyone closer to knowing his identity than she? Her only suspicions were with Telford's new neighbor. Even that was circumstantial. He hadn't done anything out of the ordinary. Scary pumpkins are certainly not unusual on Halloween. There was no peculiar activity at his house since moving in. A glowing basement window? Not much to report. Grandmom and Queen

Mab would expect much more from her if she were to contribute to the gentry. After all, her name meant Elf Ruler. She wondered what meanings were hidden in the names of others, especially those who were close to her. She must add that to her list of books to look for at the library. Ignatius Porteur had been somewhat forthcoming at his introduction, however. She remembered him saying, 'The fire of the house is my place to collect, and I am the gatekeeper of the entrance. My stature is small, but my tasks are without bounds'. Perhaps his name means Gate Keeper of the Fire. Settling back into a comfortable chair by the fire with her chili, she realized she wouldn't gain the trust or respect of anyone with immature and novice guessing.

Work at Crabapple Corner kept Aubrey's mind off of Mike at least until the party. Things were running smoothly at the garden shop. Christmas trees, wreaths, and roping were delivered. It felt as if the holidays were in full swing.

The dress should arrive in the next day or so, giving her enough time to find something else if it didn't work out. She went straight home from work the next few days to help out Merle at the inn. Lisa and Kristi stayed until Tuesday afternoon. Aubrey was sad to see them go. They were bubbly and full of positive energy. The inn could use more of that. Even Grandmom smiled when they were about.

NOVEMBER 6

With the inn empty once again, Aubrey was able to go to the library on Thursday, after work. The same librarian greeted her with a smile, and showed her to the nonfiction section.

"Hello, Jenny. I'm hoping this will help me secure a library card the right way. It hadn't occurred to me that I did have my mail from St. Louis forwarded. Will this bank statement do?"

"Yes, of course. It was nice of you to bring it in, but not necessary. The card you have is a permanent one. What might you be looking for today?"

"I want to be more helpful with the inn's garden this coming spring. Are there books on horticulture?"

"Yes, there is a nice variety. It is one of our most popular sections, because of all of the self-proclaimed gardeners in Ste. Germaine. Are you hoping to get the garden at the inn back into shape?"

"That's my plan. I'd like to use some of the skills I acquired at the Botanical Garden in St. Louis."

"I'm sure your grandmother would like to see new life in that garden. People around town wondered why the outside of the inn seemed a bit run down."

"Well, no need for anymore worry. I'm going to be around for a while. Also, business is picking up at the inn. We're looking forward to decking the halls. Merle and I have even discussed opening the inn back up to afternoon tea, as well."

"That would be wonderful. I know the ladies in town have missed that. Here at the library, we have a community bulletin board for our members. If you'd like to advertise tea time at your inn, you are welcome to do so."

"Thanks. That would be very helpful. My friend, Telford, had given me a tour of the library, but I don't recall seeing the American Literature section."

"Of course. It's just over there. You'll find horticulture right around the corner from that. Let me know if you need anything else."

"I will."

Aubrey wished she had not been so harsh to judge her at their first meeting. Now to research the Hawthorn... She found a lot of designing books, which seemed appropriate for Ste. Germaine. She could have spent hours looking through those as a jump-start to her spring endeavor, but learning about the Hawthorn tree must be her focus. The only prior knowledge she could bring to today's table was given to her by Merle in a brief conversation they had when she first arrived at the inn. He said the one in their garden was one of the more common Hawthorns, and was considered the single seeded variety. That was not much to go on, but to her benefit, Aubrey was excited to do the necessary research. And more excited to feel a part of the gentry and its mission.

Three books stood out that might provide useful tidbits of information: Trees of North America, Trees and Their Properties, and The Mystery of Trees. Surely, this would be a good start, she thought, and headed to one of the quiet rooms near the elevators. Seclusion meant no children, but more importantly, no curious townspeople. She was able to sit at a small table facing the door. Her intention, on this visit anyway, was not to check out any books that would leave a trail about the Hawthorn tree. Thinking ahead she brought a satchel containing pens and a legal pad. After a few good hours of uninterrupted research, the librarian popped in to check on her.

"Are you still doing alright?"

"Yes, I'm getting some very good ideas for the look of our spring garden."

"It probably doesn't hurt that you're working for Betty and Martin at Crabapple Corner, does it?"

"You are right about that. They run a very nice business. I consider myself lucky to be a part of it."

"Maybe we'll run into each other when my kids and I pick out our tree."

"I'm sure we will. How did you know that I work there?"

"Just shared information, that's all. I'll let you get back to it."

Things were so different in a small town. Back in St. Louis there was at least some sense of privacy. In Ste. Germaine, however, there didn't seem to be any at all. Slowly, but surely, she was getting used to it. No wonder Grandmom's warnings about sharing what was on the paper were so stern.

Aubrey filled several pages of the notepad with curious findings from the first two books. Some of the notes were as follows:

Single-seeded Hawthorn
  • Crataegus monogyna

- 30 feet tall
- Good to poor soil
- Bloom: white in clusters
- Season: late May
- Fruit: (haws) dull red, persisting all winter, jellies and jams
- Petals: salads
- Extra:
  - Called Maythorn and Motherdie
  - Firewood-provides good heat and little smoke
  - Associated with fairies in Ireland

She read through some of her notes and realized how proud Merle would be. There was so much to know just about one tree in their special garden. For now, she had to keep all of this a secret. Filled with panic she remembered Grandmom telling her she must never keep a diary or journal. If not for these notes, how was she ever to remember details about the Hawthorn tree? She promised herself that she would read them over and over until she was sure they were securely tucked away inside her being. Then she would burn them in the kitchen's wood-burning stove. No trace left for sure. That was the best solution.

She was finally ready to open the last of the three books... The Mystery of Trees. She turned to the Hawthorn, and wrote quickly as she skimmed the pages.

Planet: Venus and Mars
Symbolism: Purification
Birds: Blackbird, Owl
Medicinal Properties:
- Reduce blood pressure
- Mild sedative
- Treat migraines and insomnia
Magical Properties: (Her skimming turned into deep reading for complete understanding.)

- Cleanses negativity of the heart
- Stimulates love and forgiveness
- Helps prayers reach heaven
- Wands made of its wood hold much power

- Sitting under it on May 1st-you will be whisked away to the fairy underworld
- Falling asleep beneath one may result in fairy anger
- Never, ever damage one

Protection Spell:
- If you seek protection from a person, write his or her name on a piece of paper. Wrap it in thorns collected from the tree. Then bury it in the ground at the base of the same tree.

Other Facts
- The Mayflower name came from this tree
- The thorns were said to be the thorns that formed the crown of Jesus Christ
- With Oak and Ash trees, the Hawthorn forms the fairy triad
  - This triad creates a thin veil between the worlds and fairies are more easily seen

These findings, she thought, were too good to be true. Oh, Grandmom was such a wise woman. If only she could own this book. What other trees held such powers? Powers that pertained to the half-fairy she was... Not only did she have her hourglass and knife, she now had the magic of the Hawthorn tree.

Each book was carefully returned to its original location. In the American Literature section she found a book entitled the Life and Genius of Nathanial Hawthorne. She grabbed a copy of Gone With the Wind from the fiction section. These would leave no trail to the gentry and its mission.

NOVEMBER 7

As she drove home from the library, her mind was focused on the Dark Elf. Would it be possible to persuade him to fall asleep beneath the tree? Were the berries really strong enough to slow his heart and sedate him? But there were no berries at this time of year. What about the branches? From those could she fashion a magic wand? But that would mean harming the tree. So much to think about and worry upon.

"Aubrey, a package arrived for you today. It is in the entry hall."

"Thank you, Merle. Is Grandmom here?"

"Yes, you'll find her in the parlor going over some papers."

"Hello, Grandmom. How was your day?"

"More importantly, how was yours?"

"It was pretty uneventful. Betty says I'm whipping the place into shape. We sold a few Christmas decorations. Oh, I've forgotten to tell you. I hope it's okay that I've invited Telford and his mother to our small Thanksgiving dinner. Will that be alright?"

"Yes, just let Merle know so he can shop and prepare accordingly."

"I will. Telford should let me know sometime this weekend. They don't seem to have anyone else."

"You are kind in nature, dear Aubrey. Just don't let it stand in your way of right judgment when the time comes."

With Grandmom, even the most casual of conversations could turn into a hidden message complete with innuendos and life lessons.

"Grandmom would you like to see what arrived for me today?"

"Yes, of course."

"It's a dress I hope I'll be wearing to a dance. A nice gentleman came by the garden shop for hay the other day. One thing led to another. Now I'm going to a fancy party on his estate."

"Aubrey Bhaltair, you must be more forthcoming in the goings on of your life!"

"What do you mean, Grandmom?" she asked while holding the dress against her waist.

"I mean, perhaps you didn't know this, but I, too, am going to the party."

"Are you sure, Grandmom? I don't know the man's last name. I could find out by looking into the records at the garden shop."

"No need. His last name happens to be Reynolds. That is a very lovely dress."

"Thanks. And by the way…you kept your invite from me, as well. I've told you who my date is. What about yours?"

"Why, Merle, of course. He cleans up quite nicely. You'll see. Now upstairs you go. I'm sure you are excited to see how your new dress fits."

The dress fit perfectly. She tried it on with her heels first, then the cowboy boots. She quickly decided that the heels were no longer necessary. Her short-waisted jean jacket with her black ankle boots would provide the right combination to pull off the ultra casual look that Mike had mentioned. Mike Reynolds. Though she knew Grandmom could afford the pricey donation, she wondered why she would want to attend the dinner. While Aubrey adored Merle, she was surprised that Grandmom was going with an employee.

NOVEMBER 10

Just after lunch, Aubrey received a text from Laura. It read: 'Telford is riding his bike over…is that okay?'

Aubrey responded: 'Absolutely.'

Telford sped up to the side driveway and pushed his bike around to the back porch. Aubrey greeted him at the door.

"Thanks for letting me come over."

"Of course… anytime that I'm home, and it's great that your mom and I are texting."

"Yeah. She said it gives her peace of mind."

"So, why aren't you in school?"

"We're off today for Veteran's Day. Mom said I could come over if I had all of my homework finished. There wasn't much. I just needed to double check my math problems."

"Do you need any help? I could look them over for you."

"No, that's okay. But I do have some good news to tell you!"

"What's that?"

"First, mom said she would love to come for Thanksgiving. She wanted me to ask about the time and what to bring."

"That's great. I'll talk with Merle and let her know. I'm so glad the tack shop is closed for the holiday."

"Me too. Plus, that's not all of my news. Mom said that because my grades have been so good this school year, she might get me a phone for Christmas. I told her I could wait, but she said her holiday bonus might cover it."

"That's wonderful. Oh, I forgot to ask... what did she think about your spiffy new wallet?"

"She loved it, and gave me all the same rules you did. It's like I have two moms! Plus she gave me two more dollars. I'm keeping it safe in my treasure box. I think I heard your phone buzz."

Aubrey pulled her phone from her back pocket. It was a text from Mike Reynolds. No words just an emoji of a bouquet of flowers. She smiled and stuck it back into her pocket.

"Mom said you're going to the Veteran's party out at that big ranch next Saturday."

"I am. His name is Mike Reynolds. He bought some hay from the garden shop so I delivered it for him. I don't think it's like a date or anything. Maybe just a thank-you dinner."

"You know you're only fooling yourself, don't you?"

"What do you mean?"

"He's new in town, you're new in town. You're both nice people. At least Mom says so."

"Does she know Mr. Reynolds?"

"Yeah, but only because he needed someone to help with the horses for the hay ride. He had two beautiful mares delivered to the ranch. Mom's boss says she's the best one to handle the horses, so she'll be working that evening. And I get to help out. I've never really been around horses. But they must be pretty great because mom loves them so much."

"That is awesome news. We might get to see each other. If you don't have to work the entire evening maybe we can go on the hayride together. I'm sure Mr. Reynolds will be tending to his guests most of the time."

"I wouldn't count on it. Mom says Mr. Reynolds is rich enough to have all kinds of hired help. Let's go throw pennies into the wishing well!"

NOVEMBER 15

Grandmom wore a garnet red floor-length gown with matching jacket. Clear crystals were sewn at the neckline. With her silver purse and heels, Aubrey had never seen her grandmother look so beautiful. Her ruby and diamond earrings matched the bracelet dangling form her wrist.

Merle, in a slick black tux, appeared at the door announcing, "Nola Bhaltair, you are absolutely stunning. Our car is here. Remember, we are stopping to pick up a bottle of wine for Mr. Reynolds."

"Merle, please speak with the driver. I want to chat with Aubrey for a moment."

"Of, course."

"What is it?" Aubrey asked.

"Dear Aubrey. You look like a young woman with a smiling heart this evening. It has been a while since you've been treated well, or even been out on a date. But make no mistake, we cannot afford for you to let your guard down. Most of the people you meet this evening will be strangers. Our plan requires heightened senses. We are to make note of anything or anyone that doesn't appear quite the norm. Your purse is small, I see, but I trust it has all the right props for a girl to keep her nose powdered properly."

"I've made sure of it Grandmom. And I do understand my responsibilities. I've been working really hard. A simple evening out will not set my efforts back."

"That is good. Very well, then. It looks like there are now two cars waiting in front of the inn. Yours is the brown one. This will certainly give Mrs. Emerson something to talk about with her friends tomorrow. Enjoy yourself. I will lock up. If we need to, we'll talk later on."

"Grandmom, will you tell Merle I think he looks very handsome this evening?"

The evening was cool. A few townspeople had already begun putting up Christmas lights. They looked faded through the heavily tinted windows of the limo.

"Driver," Aubrey started, "may I put my window down to see how some of the houses are decorated?"

"Of course, ma'am. I'll direct some heat back there just in case."

His voice sounded vaguely familiar, but she wasn't quite sure from where. She could see only his eyes in the rear view mirror.

"Do we know each other?" She asked.

"I don't think so. No, wait! You work at the garden shop. I bought pumpkins from you for Halloween."

"That's right. Did you move into that house over on Third Street?"

"I sure did. How did you know?"

"I'm new to town also, and it's the only house I have seen a for sale sign in front of. You live by my friend Telford.

"Yeah, I expected to see him on Halloween, but he never showed."

"He spent the evening with me. Kids his age don't really dress up and go out anymore."

"Ah."

"So do you work for Mr. Reynolds full time?"

"No I work for a car service. They send me here and there. I kind of like driving people around. Not that I'm lazy, but it helps me pay my bills and I'm getting to know the town. It looks like we're here. I'm supposed to drop you off at the main entrance to the house. It's a pretty fancy set up if you ask me."

"I'm sure it's just one of many well-to-do estates in Ste. Germaine. Will you be taking me home? If not, my grandmother, who is also attending, will have a car."

"You're my last fare this evening. My directions from Mr. Reynolds did not include the trip home."

The man got out of the limo and rounded the car to open Aubrey's door. Before he managed to get there, the door slowly opened. Mike Reynolds had appeared from nowhere. What a handsome man, she thought. She was drawn immediately to the beautiful tie, and narrow cut of his black suit. There were diamond cufflinks at his wrists. Finally, the cowboy boots were the perfect finish to a finely dressed man. The boots were the deepest shade of red, matching one of the details in his Jerry Garcia tie.

"You made it. Welcome." Mike helped Aubrey from the limo by holding her hand ever so gently. "I've got it from here, Dillon. Thanks for the special delivery," he continued as he handed the man folded up bills. "I'll make sure Miss Bhaltair makes it home safely."

"Hi," Aubrey managed to say. "This is already proving to be an exciting evening. Did you know that my grandmother and our innkeeper will be in attendance this evening?"

"I did know that. But, my party planner sat you apart. Said something about it making for new conversations among new friends."

"That makes sense. Also, I know Laura, who will be handling the horses."

"Yes, that's right. Her son cannot say enough nice things about you. Laura seems genuinely thankful that you have taken him under your wing."

"We came into each other's lives at just the right time."

"Sometimes things happen like that. Fate, right?"

"I suppose."

"You look perfectly beautiful this evening. You make 'ultra casual' a real thing. Love your boots."

"Thanks, I bought them in St. Louis."

Aubrey and Mike made their way to one of the large barns. It was red and about thirty feet tall. Inside there were three long tables decorated as you would see in a fine restaurant; goblets, white linens, fresh flowers. A DJ, tucked in the hayloft, played soft music, while people were mingling near a bar and what appeared to be a dance floor.

"I have a couple of final details to attend to. Do you think you'll be okay for just a few more minutes?"

"I'll be just fine. Before the evening gets underway would it be okay if I went to say hello to Telford and his mother?"

"Absolutely. They should be in the other barn, just to the right. I'll see you in a bit."

Aubrey found the barn easily. Peeking inside she saw Laura brushing one of the horses. She looked so happy. Telford was sweeping and talking with a barn cat perched just above on a crossbeam.

"You two certainly look at home."

Telford beamed. "Hi, Aubrey. Look! Mr. Reynolds has a cat! He said it came with the house."

"No, you can't have one." Laura smiled at her happy young son.

"Mom, I promise not to ask for a cat until you get a horse."

Aubrey chimed in, "That sounds like a really tight promise. I just wanted to say hi. Mr. Reynolds said there were still a few minutes before dinner. Oh, Telford, you might see Grandmom and Merle later on. They will be here, as well."

"I probably will, since I get to ride in the front of the wagon, and help mom guide the horses on the hayrides. This is going to be a great night!"

"I'll see you two later on."

As she walked back to the main barn, Aubrey noticed a dark brown limo turning to the back of the main house. Hers was the only brown one she had seen. She wondered, why was Dillon still here?

Aubrey was not much of a drinker, but it was fun to walk around with a martini in her hand. Now that's an ultra casual drink, she thought to herself.

"There you are." She heard Mike's voice behind her. "Come, it's time to sit for dinner. It means so much to me that you are here. As you can see, financially, this is a very successful event for the Veteran's. Emotionally, I'm kind of a wreck. I have to give a speech later."

All at once a loud commotion could be heard coming from the main house. Aubrey tightly clutched her purse. What is happening? Two men came running into the barn shouting for Mr. Reynolds. "Come quickly, Mike. There's been a horrible accident at the house. We've called 911, but you must come at once."

A few guests shouted that they were doctors and hurried toward the two men. Mike squeezed Aubrey's hand and stood up shouting, "Everyone stay put until we know it is secure. Police are sure to be on their way. Until I know more the safest place to be right now is this barn. A few of you men bolt all of the windows and doors."

Mike motioned for the guests that were doctors to go with him and the doors and windows were locked tight behind them as he had directed. Aubrey looked around the barn. Some of the guests huddled together, while others ate appetizers, showing a mixed bag of emotions. She fell somewhere in the middle. How could anyone have an appetite? Whether or not the contents of her purse would be of any help, knowing she had her knife was of some comfort. Her hourglass necklace was of no use at the estate. Worried about Telford and his mom, Aubrey sent Laura a text. She responded saying that she, Telford, and two others were on lock-down in their barn. The men they were with were communicating with someone at the main house. Grandmom and Merle stayed seated. Peculiar though, Merle was holding her grandmother's hand. Who was it that said they thought Merle had a crush on Grandmom? She couldn't remember. There was not another familiar face at the event. Grandmom nodded from the other end of the table. Perhaps she was trying to tell Aubrey that danger was not as immanent as the others perceived. It did seem like a grave situation, however. There was no mistaking that. There was also no mistaking that Aubrey had seen the brown limousine going to the back of the house. Though time seemed to be standing still there in the barn, everything was moving so fast without explanation.

Sirens could be heard approaching the estate. One of Mike's employees had taken up a spot in the loft next to the DJ. There was a small window that faced the house. He yelled down to the guests, "Two police cars and an ambulance are nearing the front of the house. Two more police cars are blocking the entrance. Mr. Reynolds has texted advising that we sit tight."

Aubrey went over to the bartender and asked for another martini. What could it hurt? She pulled the strap of her clutch out. It made her feel better to throw it over her head in cross-body fashion. There was no possibility of losing her purse or its contents. She noticed that Grandmom clung to her silver purse in the hand not occupied by Merle. Did her grandmother have her own magical artillery? Did Grandmom and Merle love each other?

A huge knocking came upon the entrance to the barn. One man turned to the guests announcing, "It's Mr. Reynolds. Everyone stay calm. He would like to speak with us."

Mike entered the barn. From behind him appeared Telford, Laura, and several other people. Aubrey hurried toward Telford and his mom. There was shouting from all corners of the barn.

"My most sincere apologies," Mike spoke loudly, "for the obvious worry and concern that has resulted from a truly unfortunate event. I regret to inform you that one of my valets has suffered a fatal heart attack. If we could take a moment... Mike bowed his head. Most of the guests did the same. There was an uncanny silence throughout the barn.

Mike continued on, "I will completely understand if anyone would like his or her contribution refunded. While he was only employed for a short while, he will be remembered as a lovely man. My understanding is that he did not have life insurance. I will see to it that his wife and son are taken care of. In the meantime, the evening will carry on. Our fundraising efforts will not be impeded. The money raised this evening is already on its way to the Veteran's benefit fund. You may choose to stay or go, but the evening will go on. The main course will be served within the hour, and Miss Laura and her son, Telford, will be ready for hayrides just after. Those who are waiting for a hayride may enjoy time at the bonfire. Again, my heartfelt apologies for this. Our dear Lord has a way, and we are not at liberty to understand His workings. Now, I must excuse myself and give my very sweet date a quick kiss before she loses interest in me all together."

Mike made his way toward Aubrey. "How are you holding up?"

"You handled everything so smoothly. Are you sure it was a heart attack?"

"Of course. Why do you ask?"

"Mike, isn't there a bit of mystery in what happened tonight?"

"My men, the help, everyone involved reported things to me just as they occurred. Why should there be such intrigue?"

"It's not that. Will his wife request an autopsy? Won't your insurance company do an investigation, since he died here?"

"Our first date is not as I had hoped."

"Mike Reynolds, once a man is pronounced dead, being on a date goes on the back burner. You may have asked for a few moments of silence, but my mind went straight to suspicion. And for the record... the limo you sent for me...."

"Yes, what about it? I ran into someone at the bank that recommended that service."

"The same car that dropped me off at the front of your house," Aubrey took a deep breath.

"Yes, he was instructed to do so."

"I saw it going to the back of the house, later, after he should have left the estate."

"What are you getting at?"

"Could the driver of my limo somehow be responsible for the death of your valet?"

"Aubrey, my understanding is that you are a horticulturalist, not a mystery writer. Where is all of this coming from?"

"Maybe I have a tendency toward big city drama. I realize this is a small town, but anything is possible. How well did you know your valet?"

"You might be surprised, but I don't know anyone in this town very well. It was very important to me that the Veteran's fundraiser be a quick success. So I went at it in a steadfast manner. I hired people, created an event, and raised money. I didn't worry about anything or anyone getting in the way. I'm embarrassed to say that's how I've been running my life these past few years. Right now, I want to make sure the Veteran's feel like this event is truly for them. In just one half hour from now, a bus will arrive with thirty Vets that reside in Ste. Germaine. They will be honored at the bonfire lighting. Some will choose to go on the hayride. Others, will gather round and hopefully be able to share their stories. My stomach is in knots. You might have a news reporter agenda, or just want to know the answers to questions. I'm just one man. A man who wanted to make a difference, and just happened to meet a lovely woman with a bright smile. At the end of this evening you may hate me, but at the end of this evening, I'm hoping to fetch a kiss and hold your hand."

Mike reached for Aubrey's hand. Just then, Merle spoke up, "Aubrey, Grandmom is glad to see you are holding up so well. She would like for you to be on the same hayride as us. Will young Telford be able to join us?"

"Merle, I am so glad you are here this evening. Going on the hayride together is a great idea. Hopefully carrying on with the evening will not appear to be insensitive. We will see Telford, as he will be with his mom the whole time. At this point, sitting down for dinner will create a sense of normalcy. And let's keep Laura and Telford close. Mike, would you mind checking on them?"

"Of course."

Mike returned, and was talking to another guest. After waiting for a few moments, Aubrey touched him on the shoulder. Mike turned toward her with a look of sadness.

Aubrey began, "When someone dies, it is understandable that emotions are running in fourth gear. You've had a difficult job this evening and you've managed it well. In fact, without really knowing you, I'm very proud of how you've handled it. While this is an extremely sad and unfortunate event, I believe you've gained the respect of a great many people. That isn't easy to do, especially with complete strangers. You were a real leader this evening."

"That means a lot. Why does everything seem so messed up?"

"Listen, Mike, one of the most important things you will learn about me is... I look on the bright side of things while wearing rose colored glasses. You're not dead, so no whining allowed. Someone is dead, and there is a mystery at bay. What can we do about it? I'm not sure. But what I do know is ... if you kiss me quick, go about your business, no one will know, but me."

Mike Reynolds took Aubrey Bhaltair into his arms and kissed her. In a pixie dust world it lasted forever.

"Sir," came a voice from behind them, "they're serving the main course. The cooks made sure to not let the chicken dry out. One of the servers is quite shaken up and has asked to go home early. She has been cleared by the police detective, but would like your blessing as well."

"Thanks for the heads up. I'll be right there." He turned back to Aubrey. "If things go well, I'll look for you as dinner is ending."

"Please don't make me a priority. I'm a big girl, and can take care of myself. Though, enjoying the hayride together would be nice."

"If I don't show up, please don't wait for me."

"No worries. I've already promised Grandmom that I would ride with her."

There was now a vacant chair across from Grandmom and Merle. Aubrey moved the half-eaten salad to the side.

"There you are Aubrey. I see Mr. Reynolds caught up with you. As the leader of our gentry it is my job to issue warnings as I see fit. It is my opinion that you are moving too quickly with him. Springtime may seem like a long way off, but until we know the identity of Wild Edric, you… we cannot be too careful. He could be anywhere and anyone. Has he even arrived to Ste. Germaine? No one knows. Until Wild Edric has been defeated, and this means death, I strongly suggest that you keep your eyes open, your mind focused, and your heart surrounded by doubt. No infatuation is worth your own peril. Not heeding my warnings would be a true showing of selfishness."

"Grandmom, I understand. It is much too soon, as you say to open up myself to anyone. Even if he is charming."

"Aubrey, the devil himself can be charming."

"Grandmom, I apologize, but I'd like to change the subject."

"As you wish."

"Aubrey," Merle spoke up, "I'm delighted that Telford and his mother will be joining us for Thanksgiving."

"Please let me help with the shopping and meal preparations. I'm sure Telford would love to go the store with me."

"I'll let you know when I've put a list together."

"Will there be pie?"

They both smiled just a little.

Aubrey continued, "Grandmom, there's a woman at the end of our table on my side. She seems very familiar. Do you recognize her?"

"I do not. It's possible that she would appear quite differently if it were not for her gown, hair-do, and make up."

"You're probably right."

Their dinner was served. Aubrey picked at her chicken and potatoes. Merle and Grandmom went on with dinner, smiling and chatting, as if nothing had happened.

Sure, thought Aubrey, they probably have found

their soul mates in one another. And why are they keeping it a secret? Out of respect for the two of them she would not ask until a more fitting time. Apple fritters were served for dessert. She broke off a small piece, wrapped it in a napkin, then tucked it into her purse. She knew Ignatius would love finding a treat by the stove later on.

A large wagon filled with bales of hay passed the double doors of the barn. It was pulled by two beautiful horses. Telford and Laura sat together in the front to guide the horses. Mike was nowhere to be seen, so Aubrey exited the barn with Grandmom and Merle. Most of the guests headed toward the blazing bonfire, where a few were already roasting marshmallows. She, Grandmom, and Merle boarded the hayride. It was an uneventful trip around the estate, but she could see that Telford was having a great time. When they arrived back at the barn for the second trip around the estate, she saw that same brown limousine heading down the long driveway. She watched as it turned left away from town. Maybe that's where the company's business or garage was located. She wondered if Mike was satisfied with the conclusion made by the EMTs. Would there, in fact, be an autopsy? For heaven's sake, did Grandmom have a hand in this? What if the valet had been an 'unwanted member of society'? It was obvious that Grandmom had zero tolerance for those who want to harm others. She couldn't, however, fit a pie into her purse. But… if Aubrey, just finding out about her half-fairy status, had two magical options… how many might Grandmom, or even Merle have at their disposal? She possessed only a micron of magic in the world of fair folk. Could she fashion a wand out of the wood from the Hawthorn tree without harming it? Was that what Grandmom expected of her? What respectable fairy wandered about without a wand, anyway? And what about all of the tales that included fairy dust that she had read? A knife and an hourglass would have to do, she supposed. Thinking about her powers, until that moment, took her mind off Mike Reynolds.

"Sorry I wasn't able to jump on the first wagon out. In all

of the excitement, I misplaced my speech. Thankfully a cook found it in the kitchen. Are you still up for a ride?" Mike asked sitting down beside her.

"I am."

The hayride set off on its second trip. It was approaching nine o'clock. Mike Reynolds delivered a very touching tribute to the veterans, then rejoined Aubrey.

"Telford seemed glad that you rode along. You sure are a good friend to him."

"I haven't had that many friends in my life. He just made things seem natural. His mother, Laura, is a very nice person. You have no idea how much it means to her to be around your horses. Is it possible that you might need her on a more regular basis?"

"If you hadn't told me, I wouldn't have known about her love for horses. The owner at the tack shop just said she was the best person for the job."

"Telford has told me that she had a horse when she was younger, and because of money, can't afford one now. It's a shame when someone cannot truly live out his or her passion. Were you able to see her interact with the horses earlier?"

"I didn't. But shouldn't we be focusing on you and this beautiful fall evening?"

"Mike, I feel I mislead you with that small kiss. In St. Louis, I was in a very serious relationship that ended quite badly. In fact, the breakup caused me to relocate back here to Ste. Germaine. Would it be okay if we took things slowly? I'll understand if you say no."

"You are hiding something, and that was no small kiss. It meant something, and now you mean something to me."

"But we barely know each other. There is no doubt that you are charming, handsome, and quite debonair... did I mention charming? However, I promised myself that I would not jump naively into another relationship. Please respect my wishes. And if you can't then that may have been our first and last kiss."

"Aubrey, something has gotten into you. But I am a man of patience and grace. I may have charm, but you have gifts that you are unaware of. I will respect your wishes. After this evening, I will wait for you to reach out to me... as they say, I will follow your lead."

"Thank you for understanding."

Telford appeared wearing a great big grin. "Did you like it? It was fun, wasn't it?"

"It sure was. Can you sit with us by the fire?"

"Nope, I'm still on the clock. Mom is going to give me another few dollars if I help her wipe down the horses. She says it's important for them to feel groomed and appreciated after working. I'm learning a lot from my mom."

Telford ran to the front of the wagon and jumped in beside Laura. He took one of the reigns and together they guided the wagon to the other barn.

"I see what you mean. She certainly does have a soft spot for them. Perhaps I could use her part-time in the stables. Having Telford around would do me some good. Right now I have only one man seeing to the barns. He grandfathered in with the estate. Very reliable fellow, but not much spark. His wife passed away from cancer a few months ago. A true devotion to the horses might be contagious. I'll speak with him tomorrow."

"What did you mean about having Telford around?"

"Sometimes I take life too seriously. He is a very likable boy. Plus he's your best friend. If I could get him to put a good word in for me, maybe months might turn into weeks. I never was any good at waiting for something I want."

Aubrey smiled shyly. "Mike, can you have one of your workers make sure that Laura and Telford make it home safely?"

"Why are you so concerned?"

"I still have my suspicions about the driver you sent for me. To add to that, he lives right next to Laura and Telford."

"The company came with good references and they spoke highly of their driver."

"I'm sure it did, but something doesn't feel right."

129

"You have more to say and ask than the police did! What is up?"

"It's as if you think I'm being unreasonable."

"Well, this is behavior I would expect if someone had died at your inn. Why do you seem on such high alert? It feels like you're interrogating me. By the way, what happened to the positive girl wearing rose colored glasses?"

"Oh, Mike. I'm very sorry. You are a good listener. I'll give you that. Let's just call it an evening."

There was mostly silence on their drive back to the inn. Aubrey could not help but let Mike hold her hand. How could she deny him that? Surely she wasn't holding the hand of Wild Edric. Oh, Grandmom, she thought, your stern orders have placed doubts in my head. Her intensions, to be sure.

"Laura is supposed to text me when they arrive home. Thank you for making sure of their safety."

He went around to open her door. She had never had any-one take such care of her...look at her that way. Grandmom had placed a very large dilemma in front of her.
They held hands as he walked her to the front door.

"I'm going to call the car service on Monday and ask about the possibility of a second brown limo. That might put your mind at ease."

"Thank you, Mike. And thanks for all of the fun parts of the evening. I had a very nice time, in spite of someone dying. Most of all you made me feel very safe."

They hugged and Mike got back into his car. Aubrey waited until he was out of sight to enter the inn. All of a sudden there was a motion and rustling of leaves from the corner of the porch.

"Tara, what on earth? You startled me!"

"I'm sorry, Star. Waiting for you or Grandmom to arrive home has been horribly difficult."

"Why? What is so important?"

"There was a man milling about the property tonight. Grandmom warned me that Wild Edric might have second sight so I had to remain out of view."

"Did you get a good look at him?"

"He had very dark hair, kind of tall. That's all I could tell from up in the Elder tree."

"What time was he here?"

"It must have been about two hours ago."

"Could you see the car at all?"

"Only that it was a dark color. Nothing else. I'm sorry. It was too far from the tree for me to see it very well. At first I thought he might be a burglar, but he did some peculiar things."

"Like what?"

"In turn, he touched each of the three large trees, walking between them. He did this several times. Then he tried the door to the greenhouse. The main house was of no interest to him."

"What else?"

"When he couldn't get into the back house where Merle lives, he tried getting into the shed."

"Oh, Tara. Were you frightened?"

"Not at all, mostly curious. I felt helpless, though."

"Why?"

"Grandmom said Edric couldn't be defeated by just one of us. I could have done something, but that would have brought attention to me."

"Tara, I believe you did the right thing. I'll stay up until Grandmom and Merle return from the party. Are you comfortable with me conveying to them what you saw this evening?"

"Of course."

"I have a peculiar question."

"Go on."

"When something happens in the garden, does Malvina know about it in the world below? I remember parts of the underworld mirroring life up here."

"She is connected to everything up here. Her powers are very unique. Malvina has the ability to go anywhere, listen to people without suspicion. She can even appear to be human. Whenever she leaves the underworld, without exception, she always returns to the same exact spot at the base of the Elder tree. Grandmom has made it very clear that she is off limits."

"Thank you for watching out for us. It must be a great challenge. I'll go in and wait for Grandmom and Merle to get home."

"Aubrey...did you have fun this evening?"

A great smile appeared on Aubrey's face.

"Say no more. A smile like that makes you shine like the star that you are. Night."

"Night."

Grandmom and Merle entered the front door laughing. Aubrey felt just a tiny bit jealous of them. It wasn't fair that she had to put her life on hold until Wild Edric was taken care of. She relayed what Tara had witnessed. They also discussed the death of the valet and the mystery of the limo. Grandmom was certain the stranger in the garden that evening was Wild Edric. Merle thought a motion sensor light would be a good idea and intended on having one installed tomorrow.

"See Grandmom, Mike is no longer a suspect to us."

"Did Tara say what time she saw the intruder?"

"It was about two hours ago."

"Can you, without a doubt, say that you are aware of Mike's whereabouts the entire evening?"

"No, I can't be certain."

"I think that is all for this evening, Aubrey."

"Grandmom did you or Merle have anything to do with the death of the valet?"

"Why Aubrey! That is very rude and presumptuous of you. As I've said before, just because a few people expire after eating a bite or two of pie, doesn't mean every death is at my hands. But rest assured, if someone does deserve a slice of pie I won't hesitate to serve it."

Speechless, Aubrey walked toward the kitchen. She placed the wrapped fritter behind the wood-burning stove. Making sure the doors to the inn were secured, she headed up to bed.

The days between Mike's party and Christmas went by quickly. Telford enjoyed shopping with Aubrey for Thanksgiving dinner. Laura revealed that Mike Reynolds had offered her a full time job. It meant more money, and she would have daytime hours only. Aubrey worried that Mike would tire of waiting for her. And she would not fault Laura for falling for a man so handsome and charming. Telford continued to help out around the inn, growing his at-home savings account. Aubrey promised him a Christmas shopping trip to West Park Mall in Cape. There were no more signs of a stranger on their property. Aubrey thought she had seen that familiar woman a handful of times after Mike's party. Then one day she ran into her at Annabelle's. Grandmom was wrong. She looked the same in everyday clothes.

"I'm sorry to bother you," Aubrey began "but you seem so familiar to me."

"I do hear that a lot, but I'm sure we don't know each other."

"Could I have met you in St. Louis?"

"It is frustrating, isn't it? When you just can't put your finger on something... a word, a familiar face, a memory. I must be off. They really do have the most delicious pies, here at Annabelle's, don't they?" She turned to leave, then said, "You may see me again, but be assured the answer will be the same." And off she went.

Aubrey asked Doris if she knew her name.

"No, she always pays with cash. And she only buys pies. Sorry Aubrey."

Mike did not call her, but he did send an occasional text. Mostly asking how she was doing. From time to time he said he missed her.

Aubrey stayed busy at Crabapple Corner during the holiday season. There were the trees, wreaths, and poinsettias to sell, and the website to keep up with. Martin Jr. seemed to be especially pleased with Aubrey and what she brought to his parents' business. Life was going on without incident in the town of

Debbie Nuessle

Ste. Germaine.

Part Four

DECEMBER 15

Telford wanted to buy his mother a charm bracelet for Christmas. On their trip to Cape Girardeau, Telford told Aubrey he thought his mom had a boyfriend. He reported that Mr. Reynolds had come to the house a few times to pick her up. He had never seen her so happy. The texting had stopped all together between Aubrey and Mike by then. Even though she had asked Laura and Telford to spend Christmas Day at the inn, the invitation was politely declined. Aubrey later found out that Laura and Telford had spent the bulk of the Christmas holidays with Mike at his estate.

DECEMBER 25

"It is a shame that Telford and his mother had other plans for today," Grandmom said to Aubrey.

"At least Telford and I spent time together decorating. Also, I'm glad to have the next few days off from the garden shop. No worries, and a quiet life. And it was a wonderful day with you and Merle. Maybe next year will be different."

"You don't seem yourself, my dear."

"If you must know, and perhaps you're relieved to hear the news…"

"What is it?"

"I haven't heard from Mike for a few weeks now. And I have it on good authority that he is now dating Laura. I knew it was completely unreasonable to think that he might wait for me."

"The future has not unfolded, yet."

"Grandmom, you always seem to put things so simplistically. It's easy for you to be callus to my feelings. After all, you have Merle."

"How can you fault me for putting your safety above your infatuation with a complete stranger? And as for my relationship with Merle... My dear, it is time that you learn a few more things about being part of this magical world. What you see before you is my real age. As you know, I was born in 1944, making both Merle and I old enough to make our own decisions. When and if we want to, we are able to change our age. However, we can never be older than our true age. There are parts of our underworld where fairies are always in their half-life. That is my favorite place to be. Merle and I visit there about once a week in our time. We feel young again and see familiar faces. Merle entertains by playing his panpipe. Being a Satyr he holds great musical talents. When we are dancing and singing, stories are shared. Most of all, there is no danger whatsoever. Unlike other parts of our magical underworld, there is absolutely no way for anyone without membership to gain entrance."

"If I went there would I be twelve years old?"

"No fairy under the true age of fifty is allowed membership."

"Grandmom, you're avoiding speaking about your relationship with Merle."

"We have been together for a very long time. As you know, Merle is a Satyr, which I found very intriguing from the moment we met. I will save that tale for another day. The gentle manner you have seen is true, and never wavering. Our love is unshakable. We would die for each other. In fact, he is prepared to die, if necessary, to protect the gentry. Aubrey, you will meet someone of this world or the other. Impatience will do you no good at all. I am tiring of this conversation. Please forgive me, but I must retire. Merry Christmas, Aubrey."

"Goodnight Grandmom. I want to sit here for a bit before going to bed. Merle made a nice fire in the parlor. I'll wait until it dies down. Some of my friends from St. Louis texted. I'm going to have a glass of wine and return a few messages."

Aubrey stood up to pour a glass of wine. Grandmom reached out and put her arms around her granddaughter. Aubrey could not remember the last time they shared a hug. At that very moment she missed her mom. But, why? Was there something else she missed? What was this emptiness?

Grandmom left the inn through the back door. Aubrey watched as her grandmother headed toward Merle's quarters.

Ignatius appeared. "Aubrey, I assure you, everything will be alright. Remember Brownies do not and cannot lie. Grandmom's recommendation for patience is very good advice. Your world right now is filled with silent turmoil. There are many fires burning that you cannot see. Ask yourself... would you rather have a boyfriend or save your gentry? Like Merle, I have everything at stake, and certainly will be using my strength and my power to save the world of the people I love. One day it will all become clear. Hopefully, it won't be too late."

"Ignatius, you are correct. It is very selfish of me to think of my heart before my home."

"No one deserves being hurt the way you were."

"Ignatius, how do you know what I went through?"

"Aubrey, you always have someone looking over you. In human terms it's called a guardian angel. You have your very own fairy watching over you."

"Who is it... for how long... have I seen them?"

"Your guardian is Malvina. She has been with you since you were born. Her abilities are sleek and silent. Every conversation you have ever had, she has heard. She has witnessed your every movement. There are very few fairies that can transform, transport, and stay right where they are all at the same time. Our great Queen Mab bestowed those powers onto only three fairies. I have met only one, Malvina. She is very special."

"When I saw her in the underworld, why didn't she say anything to me."

"Did she seem preoccupied when you met her?"

"In fact she did. Tara instructed me to leave her be. I was

not to communicate with her. This did not and does not make any sense to me."

"While Queen Mab has made her powers great, she has made her duties even greater. When she is not looking after you, listening, and gently guiding you, she is busy with another magnificent task."

"What is that?"

"She is keeping vigil over your twin sister, Athilda."

"What?! Whatever do you mean? I don't have a sister."

"You do, in fact. You and your sister were born as twins to your evil mother. She hated Grandmom. She hated life. But most of all she hated your father. Bad judgment and foolishness led her into a terribly dark marriage. Your mother was a half fairy, being a granddaughter of one. Both your mother and father were hoping to get part of Grandmom's gold. Pie was served and, your father died. The circumstances regarding your mother's death are a mystery. At that time, the townspeople were convinced that this property was run by the devil. And we both know that Grandmom is no devil. She simply administers justice. When you and your sister were born, just upstairs in the Flora Room, some of the more ambitious fairy hunters were already trying to dig up the garden. They claimed that hidden beneath its layers was a dark world. One man, related to that horrible proprietor of Annabelle's, dug far beneath the Elder tree. There were complications in childbirth, and against Grandmom's wishes an ambulance was called. Before both of you could be placed into the ambulance, a man appeared from the garden. He was able to grab only one baby, your sister Athilda. Still bloody from birth he placed her into an iron cage. As you know iron takes away all fairy magic. What he didn't know is that Queen Mab could grant Athilda her fairy status. While she couldn't free Athilda, she could allow her to transform into a beautiful fairy waiting for a release that might never come. Your mother never spoke of your twin. Malvina was chosen to watch over the two of you for the rest of her days. Fairies are completely selfless beings. Malvina knew that her life was decidedly one of service to others. Remember, she has the ability to be in many places at one time. When you think you recognize a familiar face while moving through town, it is Malvina. She is protecting you. At the same time, she is telling Athilda all about you, what your day is like, whether you are happy, everything. Malvina is a voice for you, on behalf of you."

"It does not make any sense that I'm just now finding out about this."

"Oh, but it does. How strong were you four months ago? And how much strength have you gained from the knowledge you have recently acquired?"

"What?"

"Before this evening, you might have fought against Wild Edric out of fear. Now, you are angry, confused, and full of family honor. If Wild Edric defeats you, he will possibly take Athilda and hold her captive forever. Quickly, without thinking, say out loud what you want to do."

"I want to free Athilda and defeat Wild Edric. I want my family to live without fear."

"There. You've said it. Family."

"But Ignatius, how can this be accomplished?"

"You must remain...."

"Patient."

"That is correct."

"Now that I know about Malvina and Athilda, can I please cross the ley lines and speak with them?"

"And to what end?"

"What do you mean?"

"It seems you've spent a great deal of time thinking about Mr. Reynolds and begrudging Grandmom. How has this facilitated defeating Wild Edric?"

"I'm embarrassed. I've done just a little research on..."

"Careful..."

"On my instructions. Other than that, I've relaxed quite a bit, thinking that I would have a better handle on things when spring rolls around."

"In the meantime, have you bettered yourself?"

"No, I haven't."

"Tomorrow you can wake up with the intention to move forward. You said you wanted your family to live without fear. Can you make that happen alone?"

"I need the gentry, don't I? I think it was Grandmom that told me each folded piece of paper was individually important. But we could not share their contents. How can we combine each strength without full knowledge of each written word?"

"That, dear Aubrey, is called trust."

"Ignatius, you are a true friend. When I came back to town, you appeared with your fun loving attitude. Please share with me your words of wisdom."

"Your heart is heavy for Malvina and Athilda. Do not worry about them. Malvina is strong and Athilda knows no other life. She thinks being looked after by a fairy friend is her life. The cage she lives within is comfortable to her. How would she know any different? Malvina has never alarmed her or caused her to feel that she is living a desperate life anymore than a beautiful caged bird does not know the freedom of flight."

"My heart feels broken."

"A broken heart is a heart open to possibilities. Wise Telford gave you the gift of a beautiful fairy you will never meet. She sits silently. This may, also, be the destiny of Athilda. As you sleep and dream tonight, sweet Aubrey, may your slumber be filled with patience and peace."

Holding back her tears, Aubrey spoke, "Will Athilda ever be released?"

"That is unknown. If she is released from her iron cage, her whole world will change. Remember, Wild Edric has had much time to plan the demise of our underworld. His plans will be intricate, his methods will be mad, and his goal is to personally pluck each shimmering wing from every fairy he can. Each magical mound will be blown to bits, each mist and moor will be filled with contamination. There will be no sparkle, no twinkle, and no magic. Of course, this is one gentry at a time. And if he can destroy the gentry under Grandmom's rule, his confidence will be high. It is no secret that he is angered by the fairy world and his revenge will bestow mayhem upon the magical innocence of our underworld. My not being able to tell a lie has gotten the best of me. It truly is time for bed."

Aubrey knelt down and fell into Ignatius' arms. He pulled a dirty cloth from his pocket and wiped her tears. Aubrey made her way to the stairs.

"Aubrey, you are very bright. The Hawthorn tree can help you in many ways."

She had no energy to ask how he knew that Hawthorn was her word. The Flora Room felt like solitude. It was her fortress with a miniature fairy. She shook the dome and looked at it closely. Her eyes began to close... the fairy looked like Malvina, the tree was the same as the Elder. She pulled the covers up to her shoulders and waited for sleep to come.

A rapping came upon her bedside window. It was Tara. Aubrey let her in.

"You are over thinking all of this."

"Tara, I don't know how much more I can take tonight."

"Oh, sure, Ignatius is all serious and such. All I need is a minute or two."

"What more can you possibly tell me about my life? Surely there are no more secrets."

"No, it isn't that. I'm just here to give you a pep talk."

"If you must."

"I will ask you a question, and without thinking too much, you will give the answer."

"If I can."

"You are off to a very poor start."

"What do you mean?"

"When you pulled the knife from the chest, what did I tell you? You must dig deep for a positive state of mind. Not just now, but at all times. Fairies are joyful. Now here we go... First question. Will Athilda be freed before or after the defeat of Wild Edric?"

"After."

"Why?"

"Within the cage... Athilda will stay protected.

"Very good. By the way, you were the only one with a word on your paper. Grandmom has a way of bringing out the best in a person. Testing them. Name three ways the Hawthorn tree might be used to defeat Wild Edric."

"It can slow his heart rate, encourage him to be more forgiving, and there is a protection spell."

"When was the last time you thought of those things?"

"Not recently."

"Now we're getting somewhere. You must remember that you will help the gentry defeat Wild Edric with positivity and power. Now you must make a few predictions. How can I be an asset?"

"From above with your arrows."

"Malvina...?"

"She will guard Athilda in the iron cage."

"A Dark Elf has no powers against iron. So how will Malvina protect herself if he comes near?"

"She will disappear?"

"Yes, of course. Now to Merle and Ignatius."

"My heart tells me that Ignatius is not one to inflict any sort of pain on anyone, not even Wild Edric. I see him more in a secondary role, helping Merle as needed. Merle, on the other hand, will most likely use powers that he has possibly been cultivating in his greenhouse."

"You are on the right track. Remember, we will need to work as a team. Think a bit deeper."

"Perhaps Malvina can use the protection spell of the Hawthorn tree. You might ask Merle if he has any poisonous berries on hand. The juice of the berries could be placed on the tips of your arrows."

"Let's think about one more thing. With Queen Mab and Grandmom keeping their distances, to whom will the gentry look for leadership?"

"That would be me. After all, my name does mean Elf Ruler."

"Kind of feels good to be a fairy, doesn't it?"

"It does, but right now it's easy. Have you ever dealt with the kind of wrath that Wild Edric is capable of?"

"Grandmom told you the story of a little girl who couldn't hear very well. She was bullied all of the time. This Dark Elf is just a bully with powers. As a gentry, with you in charge, we will do just fine."

DECEMBER 31

Laura and Mike hosted an elegant New Year's Eve affair for their new friends. Telford spent the evening celebrating with Aubrey. It was agreed that he could stay up until midnight and ring in the New Year, followed by a sleepover.

JANUARY 1

"Come on, Telford. Gather your things. I think your mom pulled up."

Aubrey opened the front door to the inn just as Mike Reynolds was about to knock.

"Good morning."

"Good morning, Mike. Telford is almost ready. We were expecting Laura to pick him up. Is everything okay?"

"Of course. When she can, on her day off, she loves to take the horses out for a ride. She's a real natural."

"That's nice to hear. I know how much she loves them. Telford said he enjoys the new pony. Is it Stryder?"

"Yes. He's got a while to go in the confidence department. Honestly, the way he talks, I think he'd rather spend time with you. But he knows learning to ride a horse would mean a lot to his mom. He said he wanted to surprise her."

"Hi, Mike." Telford appeared in the entry hall bundled up for the cold weather.

"Hey, sport. You all ready to go?"

"Look, Mike! Aubrey gave me this great gift. It's the Nintendo Switch. Are you taking me home?"

"No, we're headed back to the ranch."

"Can you text my mom and see if you can just drop me off at home?"

It was unclear why Laura hadn't gotten Telford a cell phone for Christmas. But Aubrey knew it wasn't her business to ask.

"Come on Sport, we'll have fun."

"Doing what? You know I'll never be able to ride a horse like my mom wants me to, and there isn't anything else to do."

"Maybe we can work on the designs for that tree house we talked about."

"Tree house?" Aubrey asked.

"Yeah, Mike says we can build a tree house in the back yard. What kind of tree is it, Mike?"

"It's an Elder tree."

"That sounds like fun." Aubrey spoke up. "Telford, come here." She gave him a small hug and said, "Sometimes it's okay just to hang out with your mom. Maybe you can play your game while she's working with the horses. Your mom really just wants to spend time with you. Being together is a really neat gift to give."

"Aubrey, don't ever get old. I like you just the way you are... my very best friend."

"Glad I metcha? You betcha! Now go on you two."

Mike didn't say goodbye or even look at her. They pulled away, leaving Aubrey on the front porch, fighting back tears. She had thought she was over him. But now she was unsure. And why would Mike build a tree house for Telford, unless he and Laura were serious about one another? She went upstairs and fell into her bed. Some Elf Ruler I am. I can't even handle heartbreak. She glanced over at the snow globe. Next to it was the book she had ordered online. It was the same one she had found at the library, The Mystery of Trees. Until now her only focus was the Hawthorn tree. She opened the book to the index, Elder tree, page 78. She turned to the section and began to add notes to the pad she kept under her mattress...

- Woodland old/mother figure
- Mistress of deepest magic
- Associated with witches
- Black heart of the earth
- A threshold crossing

Not every tree, she thought, is meant to fulfill its magical existence. After all, Mike did not live on the property when the tree was planted. Other than her being jealous, there really was no reason that Telford should not have a tree house built on Mike's estate. Wait, come to think of it, don't we have an Elder tree right here in the garden? Isn't it part of the ley line crossover? The Elder tree completes a triangle with the Hawthorn and Pine trees. Why hadn't she thought of this before? Who was it that told her about Traurig, the Pine tree? Was it Ignatius that called him their 'sad protector'?

With that, Aubrey knew it was time, as the Elf Ruler, to call a meeting.

Hey it's me, A.B. dropping in to tell you how excited I am about the introduction of Traurig, or Mr. Traurig Shutz. My reader friend, you are going to find his spirit so gentle. Traurig is one of history's finest examples of Tree Folk. Normally Tree Folk reside in thick forests, but our dear Traurig was transplanted from Austria 145 years ago. There are many tales of how he arrived here in America. The most beloved story is that of a rich Frenchman. He discovered the sapling while traveling, and his moody girlfriend requested that the tiny tree travel first class on an ocean liner to America. Ste. Germaine was one of their first stops on their way to St. Louis. On bended knee, in the garden of the bed and breakfast, his fiancée said yes to a marriage proposal. In her selfishness she requested that they abandon the sapling. This was back in 1873. The inn had just been built and needed landscaping. A true vision had not been set upon paper yet. The property caregiver was a sentimental gentleman. He planted the

tree. It was then that Traurig received his name. For more than a hundred years this sweet and gentle tree has grown in the magical garden. Malvina lived for hundreds of years in the underworld below the grounds before the garden began to take shape. It was friendship at first sight. Tara is a newer addition to their gentry. She sleeps in the Elder because of its younger and more reliable branches. But she has found a love for Traurig. His branches, while old and stiff provide the perfect perch for an expert archer such as Tara. Within the branches of all the trees, she finds safety, comfort, and a home. She and Traurig watch over the garden reporting to Grandmom and the Queen. At times, Traurig feels very, very old. But with Tara's snappy disposition and Malvina's positive attitude, Traurig comes to life each day to help with the preservation of the two worlds. Their worries are many, and their actions are guided by Queen Mab and Grandmom. The Fair Folk world is guarded by many. Sure there are bad fairies, elves, and such. But the underworld is more governing than the human world. It doesn't put up with very much of anything. In the human world grey lines are drawn daily. The same lines are crossed without recourse or consequence. The underworld is smarter. When a human says that your are banished it is with vagueness. For example, murderers can be released from prison after a short time. The underworld has rules that are meaningful. Banishment might include crawling off into darkness with only one of four limbs. The underworld is selective in judgment, and consistent. Pixie dust is meant for adornment. It is not the overall way we live.
Now back to our story... A.B.

JANUARY 2

It was a warm and much needed gathering in the kitchen of The Petit Jardin. Ignatius had a great smile upon his face. Tara perched herself atop a cabinet. Merle crossed his legs and leaned back in his chair.

Aubrey placed her knife upon the table, and began the meeting... "In turn, when I call upon you," She spoke out, "I want each of you to reveal your true self." She held up her hand as a warning that nothing else would be acceptable.

To Aubrey's surprise, Ignatius transformed into a being she had never seen before. He was neither the handsome guest at her birthday party, nor the diminutive mouse-like guardian of the hearth. Aubrey gasped as her small friend morphed into a hunched over creature. His cutting teeth grew down to his chin, and his body stretched beyond his shirt and pants. The ears of a rat replaced his simple ones and his eyes were slanted inward. Where there had once been a sensible cut of hair, now appeared a long braid down the length of his back. His entire appearance was dirty and smelled of soot. He bowed his head to Aubrey.

"My good friend, Ignatius. You may never tell a lie. Is that correct?"

"Yes, ma'am."

"As quickly as you transformed this evening..."

"Yes, ma'am."

"You must be able to draw upon your true self... all of you must. Ignatius, what can you bring to the table when we face off against Wild Edric?"

From atop the cabinet, Tara gave an approving wink.

"Oh, Aubrey, I had hoped to just remain a simple servant of the hearth. Why must I succumb to violence?"

"Ignatius, choose someone in the gentry that we can do without if they die at the hands of Wild Edric."

Ignatius looked around the kitchen. He could not choose. "Very well...I can become invisible."

"Dear Ignatius, you are holding back."

"Well, I suppose I can move about from place to place without notice."

"And..."

"If you really must know..."

"Ignatius, did you decide whom you will miss the least?"

Merle sat up and crossed his arms. A proud smile grew upon his face.

"I have the ability to control objects without touching them."

"Please explain."

"If I'm feeling a bit lazy, I can move a log into the fire. That's just an example."

"Now my dearest Ignatius, your skills will increase with the level of danger. I'm certain your exceptional powers will help the gentry. We may all die or we may all live. Does any one of us want to be left behind without the other? All of you might wonder why I chose to speak with Ignatius first. His heart is the biggest and the most blind to evil. This is not a fault, but a gift. He loves more than the rest of us. If he can draw upon his powers to defeat the Dark Elf he proves to you that it can be done. He awakens bravery in us all." She bowed to Ignatius. "Are there any questions?"

Each member of the gentry sat straight-backed and ready to be questioned. Malvina sat without notice outside, beneath the kitchen window.

"Merle, would you like to go next?"

"I must say, Aubrey, you make for a quite impressive chairman. Doubts were shared here and there. I speak for all... Shame on us."

"I bestow enormous gratitude upon Tara for awakening my responsibility as leader of this gentry. Her duties are silent, yet great, and her vision is wide." Aubrey bowed to Tara. "Tara has proven that she is ready to fight against Wild Edric the Dark Elf...Merle?"

"Yes, what would you like to know?"

"More importantly, what can you share with us? Day by day you tend to our needs, clean up after us, yet you have powers not revealed. With Wild Edric crouching in the eaves you must step it up a notch and let the rest of us know how you will contribute to his demise."

Merle fell to his knees. Hooves grew in place of his feet. Horns sprouted from his head and curved down to his goat-like mouth. Rags of leather replaced his human clothes. Long whiskers grew from his chin and his body was mostly covered in fur. Tattoos could be seen here and there. Between his two cloven hands there was a panpipe. He began to play a tune with his instrument. In a whisper he spoke, "I am torn between defender and protector. Grandmom remains silent, and has left my participation up to me. Defending the gentry means I must leave her alone."

Aubrey spoke up, "Merle, you will find your purpose, just as I have found mine." She looked around the kitchen and saw that Tara and Ignatius were sleeping.

"That will be my purpose, Aubrey. If needed, with my magic panpipe, I can cast a dreaming spell upon Wild Edric." He began to play a livelier tune causing Tara and Ignatius to come out of their sleeping trance.

"Perfect," said Aubrey. "I believe we will be ready when the time comes."

Ignatius asked, "What if we are not together when the Dark Elf approaches?"

Aubrey answered, "We must find a way to join together in the garden. Wild Edric must be taken through the ley lines between the Pine and Hawthorn trees. This will keep him a safe distance from Malvina. I have already spoken with Queen Mab. She has consented the help of a dozen fairies that are on guard near the moor. They are on high alert to conjure a mystical fog to rise from the pond, if needed. It will hover about Wild Edric, hampering his sight. We must be spontaneous, steadfast, and confident in our combined actions. His strengths and weaknesses are unknown. Catching him off guard is key."

Tara spoke up, "Aubrey, my biggest concern is… we have no idea who this creature might be. He might easily fool each of us until the very last moment. Just before his attack."

"I will not let that happen."

Aubrey grabbed her coat from the hook near the back door and went to the garden with Tara. "I'm going to sit on the thinking bench for a bit. I'm glad all of you are in my life."

Tara followed. "You are a star in my life, as well." She flittered to the top of the Elder tree.

Aubrey went to the base of Hawthorn. Using her knife she dug a small hole into which she placed a piece of paper. She then sat for a while on the thinking bench, listening to the garden. She couldn't wait to start grooming it in the spring.

"Aubrey Bhaltair...." She heard someone whispering to her. "Aubrey...."

"Who's there?" she asked.

"Aubrey Bhaltair, why have you forgotten about me?"

"I need to see you to have a proper conversation. Show yourself."

Knowing Tara was keeping a watchful eye from above gave her some comfort, but she reached for the knife in her pocket just in case.

"Aubrey...I'm right in front of you. I always have been. You even know my name."

"This game is making me a bit uneasy. If I have to, I will summon the gentry."

Tara spoke from above, "There will be no need to do that. This is Traurig, a very dear friend. Didn't Grandmom tell you about him? He is very old and wise."

"She did, a few months ago. My apologies. And, yes, I did forget about you. Is a tree considered part of a gentry?"

Traurig answered, "As much as a Satyr is, to be sure. In fact, ours is considered a very unusual gentry. Our uniqueness brings all forms of powerful magic. I listened through the window. You run a very nice meeting. Challenges, transformations, pulling the best out of each member. Your courage has grown, and you show more bravery since arriving to town. Do not be alarmed..."

"Why?"

A soft breeze floated through the garden. From branches, arms began to grow. Large toes formed from the aboveground roots at the base of Traurig's trunk. And finally his face began to appear. Very large and wise looking yellow-brown eyes seemed to hold great sadness. A drooping lopsided nose hid a portion of his mouth. Finally, whiskers made of vines grew crookedly down to the tops of his toes.

"My, my you are the most handsome tree I have ever seen.

I am not alarmed at all."

"Would you like me to demonstrate my power?"

"Yes, of course." Aubrey waited and waited. Nothing happened. "Did I miss it?" She asked.

"No, you did not. I'm sad to say that I haven't any powers. Oh, I might be good for tripping or grabbing someone up using my branch-like arms. But that completes how I might help the gentry."

"Well, I think those two actions will make fine contributions."

"I will do my best, but please know that everything a tree such as myself does, is very, very, very slow. Legend has it that once a magical tree was pushed to fierce anger. In his rage, he uprooted himself and tore down the great walls of a castle. I don't believe I can conjure such anger. Truth be told, I'm supposed to be protector of the inn's garden, but Tara is a much more suitable guardian. If it's a poem you fancy, however, writing is my real specialty. I can weave together words in fine fashion. I often dream of writing a book of spells."

"You are teaching me so much about Treefolk. A book of spells could prove to be very useful. And of course, I would love to hear your poetry. Our focus, at present, is to disarm, capture, and kill Wild Edric the Dark Elf.

"When springtime comes will you promise to give me water? That is really all I require."

"Of course I will. This garden will be beautiful once again."

"Just as it used to be when Grandmom groomed it, right?"

"Yes, you are right. Traurig, before we part I would like to know two things."

"I will tell you anything. Like Brownies, Treefolk cannot tell lies."

"Remind me again what your name means."

"Why, I am Traurig Shutz. My name is both German and Austrian. It means that I am the Sad Protector."

"Yes, now I remember. And secondly, why do you have

such grand rings upon your trunk?

"Each one represents a time when fairies or magical folk circle around me, always dancing in delight. While I'm never privy to the reason for the dancing, it is always a gleeful celebration. At times I am asked to join in the merriment. How strange it is to see a tree moving to the music of a panpipe."

"So Merle has danced in the garden?"

"Oh, yes. Dancing isn't just for fairies. When Merle is a Satyr he is quite nimble. The last ring was made the night you arrived. Merle, Ignatius, Tara, and I were celebrating just as you drove up."

"How nice to hear that the garden is a place of happiness. It is time for me to leave. Traurig, I believe this has been one of my best visits to the thinking bench. Goodnight."

"Goodnight, Aubrey."

Part Five

A DAY IN APRIL

Merle held the door to the greenhouse open as Aubrey slowly entered. It was filled with gorgeous, blooming flowers in vibrant hues.

"You look surprised, Aubrey."

"Merle I've waited so long to peek inside… I wasn't quite sure what to expect. I envisioned a workshop of poisonous berry plants, gnarled bushes, and other living instruments to aid in the defeat of Wild Edric."

"Don't let their beauty fool you. Over here we have Hemlock, the poisonous variety. Yes, it is a lovely white color, but the fruit that it bears is deadly. Quails choose the seeds of the hemlock as part of their diet, making their flesh poisonous. I'm thinking of getting a nice birdhouse for the garden. The beautiful purple bloom of the Monkshood makes it a gardener's favorite. However, all parts are poisonous, and make a lovely addition to a spring salad recipe. Vision is the first to go, then the heart is severely challenged. Death is most certainly immediate."

Aubrey could only respond, "Oh, my!"

"No need to worry. Most of the poisonous plants will be kept inside the greenhouse. Over to the left are the more common garden additions, such as daisies. You are welcome to any of those when you begin to bring the garden back to life. Now let's move on. The nectar of this lovely pink flower can lower blood pressure, induce a coma. Death is certain within six hours."

"Why would anyone think of consuming its nectar?"

"That's where creativity comes in. Nectar from the plant is a favorite among bees. Their honey can be used in tea. Don't you think I would make a sufficient beekeeper? It seems like a very relaxing job. I could go on and on. Now let's see… oh, yes this is one of Tara's favorites. It is the Spindle tree. She loves to fashion its branches into arrows. Then she dips the points in the liquid from its fruit. Within ten hours her victim exhibits symptoms of meningitis, followed by death. She has been pestering me for months, hoping it would be ready in time. Her whittling has kept her busy for the past several evenings."

"I'm very proud of you, Merle. While this is a new spin on having a green thumb, your skills have produced plants with great potential."

Aubrey's phone rang. She could see Laura was calling.

"Thanks for the tour, Merle. I can't wait to hear more. I'm going to take this outside…. Hello?"

"Aubrey, it's me, Telford."

"Hey friend, what's up? Where's your mom?"

"Everything is messed up and I'm scared. I'm up in the tree house at Mike's and the door is locked. I can't get out."

"I'll just give him a call. It will be fine. Please don't worry."

"No, you don't understand. He's the one that locked me in. I was up here playing on my mom's phone while she was working in the barn. Mike climbed the ladder and came in to tell me that there had been an accident in the barn with one of the horses and that I should sit tight. I asked if Mom was okay and he said there was no time for questions. I waited for him to be out of sight. Then I tried to leave the tree house. He must have locked the door on purpose."

"Does he know you have your mom's phone?"

"I don't think so."

"Conserve the battery of the phone and sit tight. I'm on my way over to get you out of there. I am not going to call the police just yet. This may just be a misunderstanding. You did the right thing by calling me. I love you Telford."

"I love you too… please hurry. I'm so afraid for my mom."

Aubrey took a brief second to make her decision.

"Ignatius, Ignatius!"

"Yes, ma'am. How might I serve you?"

"There is an emergency and I don't want to go alone. Can you do that human thing and ride along with me out to Mike's estate? It seems Telford has somehow gotten locked up in the tree house they built together."

"Of course. I'll meet you at the car."

The handsome upright version of Ignatius opened the car door and sat in the front seat. "Have you tried to call Mr. Reynolds or Telford's mom?"

"That's where it gets a bit complicated. Telford thinks Mike may have locked him into the tree house on purpose. And Telford has his mom's phone. To make things worse, he thinks his mom is in danger."

They made their way to the estate. Aubrey had not been there since the Veteran's Hoedown. Laura seemed to be so happy with Mike in her life. She couldn't imagine that Mike had really locked Telford in the tree house.

"Ignatius, I have no idea which tree the tree house is in, but I can tell you it is an Elder tree."

"Is that why you brought me?"

"What do you mean? I was hoping that you could somehow get the door open while I look for Laura and Mike."

"That one evening in the kitchen... when you held a meeting of the gentry..."

"Yes, what, we might not have time for conversation..."

"I held back a bit. Bravery is not my strong suit, but fire is. If I can't get the door open I may have to defeat the tree. You may not know this, but the Elder tree has a dark heart and holds very deep magic. She will sense my presence as a Brownie. There may be a struggle and the only way to defeat her, is to burn her to the ground. At the same time I must free Telford. Do you trust me?"

"Ignatius, you trusted me a very long time ago by being the first mystical being in my life. Your calmness simply made me accept and believe that there was magic. I now know there is magic everywhere. Today, good will conquer evil."

"There's the tree!" shouted Ignatius.

Aubrey drove her car off the driveway, right up to the Elder tree. She could see the tree house that had been built upon its strongest branches. Telford was leaning out of one of the side windows.

Aubrey shouted from up to him. "Ignatius is coming for you."

"Dear Aubrey, there is a great possibility that all of this is at the hands of Wild Edric, the Dark Elf."

"If so, we will have great accomplishments to toast at the end of the day. Can you drive?"

"I can figure it out!"

Aubrey tossed him the keys to her car and ran toward the barn.

Ignatius could hear her chanting: *"Weapon of power, strike evil that's near..."*

He stood at the base of the tree. From his pocket he traded the car keys for a wand. As he drew the wand, his human form began to fade. He had a spell of his own. Thrusting his wand into the trunk of the Elder tree he chanted:

"Hearth of my heart
Burn down this tree
Bring wrath and flame
So goodness can be..."

Smoldering began at the base while Ignatius nimbly climbed the tree. After climbing his way to the limb nearest the tree house window, he reached out for Telford and said, "Do not be alarmed, dear friend. I am Ignatius, the same Ignatius with whom you celebrated Aubrey's birthday. My true self is that of a Brownie, a magical creature. Come closer. I am going to touch your eyes. Tomorrow, you will have no recollection of this moment or those to come."

Ignatius touched Telford's eyes. The smoldering from

below grew into furious flames. Ignatius made his way through the branches to the door of the tree house. His wand fit perfectly into the keyhole. The door flew open, and he held Telford in his arms. They dropped safely to the ground.

"Get in and crouch down onto the floor board!" Ignatius shouted, opening the hatch to Aubrey's car. "Hand me your mom's phone.

There were no new messages. Ignatius drove to the barn. Mike and Aubrey were shouting at each other near the opened barn door. Ignatius could see a lifeless body just a few feet in.

"Aubrey!" he shouted and pulled up right next to them. She jumped in and they sped away.

Mike could be heard yelling, "He will be mine. I am to groom him. There is no stopping the wrath of Edric the Great."

Ignatius drove as fast as he could.

"Pull up in front. That's the quickest way to the garden."

Telford was moaning and incoherent. Merle came from the house to help carry him to the garden.

"It's time." That was all Aubrey said.

They gathered in the garden. Turning her hourglass, the gentry passed through the ley lines and ended up next to Malvina. Merle and Ignatius placed Telford at her feet. Aubrey once again turned her necklace. Standing near the thinking bench was Mike Reynolds with hands raised in the air. Quickly lowering his hands to his sides he became Wild Edric the Dark Elf. His jeans and shirt turned into a long black cloak. Horns appeared upon his head and fire burned in his eyes. As he reached for a long silver sword hanging at his side, Aubrey lunged at him while turning her necklace. The gentry was now facing off against Edric in the underworld, near the misty moor. Tara shot arrow after arrow into his flesh, penetrating his leather garb. The magic from the garden was working. Edric was not able to get close to Aubrey and began to stumble.

She spoke "Why did you kill Laura, and not Telford?"

"He is to be my successor. My time is almost up. Laura was in the way. It was you that was meant to die, but your beloved grandmother's wisdom got in the way. Poor sweet Laura…"

"I've had enough of this!" Aubrey shouted.

Elf form and dagger appeared all at once. Lunging at Wild Edric, she looked into his red eyes.

"You're not so much," she said, as she twisted the blade.

The poison from Tara's arrows and Aubrey's courage defeated Wild Edric the Dark Elf.

Queen Mab appeared, hovering over the moor. "Well done, Honorable Gentry of The Petit Jardin. You have proven yourselves. I will dispose of this horrible creature." She motioned to the fairies on the hillside to retrieve the remains. Together they disappeared into the moor.

It was unclear if Dillon had any connection to Wild Edric. He was never seen again. His house became vacant, and happiness bloomed at the inn. The gentry suspected he was just a pawn, a screen if you will. With Grandmom's influence, Aubrey was able to adopt Telford. He had no recall of being locked in or being rescued from the tree house. And his mother's death was ruled an accident. Aubrey left her job at Crabapple Corner, purchased a bright blue bicycle with a basket on front just the right size to tote pies. She gladly took over all responsibilities as head proprietor of the inn. She and Telford transformed the garden and business picked up. From time to time, Aubrey visited Malvina and Athilda, vowing that the iron cage would one day be opened. Telford was able to move into the attic room when Grandmom moved to the backhouse. She and Merle spoke often about retiring from… everything. In the meantime, Merle took up bee keeping, and acquired a nice collection of birdhouses. Afternoon tea was once again, a successful event at The Petit Jardin Bed & Breakfast.

A DAY IN JUNE

"Knock, knock. Can I come in?" Aubrey asked outside of Telford's door.

"Sure!"

"It's a beautiful summer day. Want to come help in the

garden?"

"Of course. Let me just put these things away."

"What do you have there?

"This is the treasure box I told you about. It holds my extra money, a few things that remind me of Mom, and some other stuff. Here's the charm bracelet we picked out for her this past Christmas. She loved the horses on it. And these are a few poems my great grandfather wrote."

"May I see them?"

"Sure, but the paper is very old."

"I'll be careful."

Aubrey read the first one to herself:

Iron bars within you hold
A fairy with a heart of gold.
Release her now to age just right
No longer keep her out of sight...

In that very instant Aubrey realized she hadn't been running from something, but to something...The Gentry.

THE END

About the Author

Debbie is a dreamer, car enthusiast, writer, poet, lyricist, jewelry maker, paper crafter, blogger, retired teacher, and family gal. Most days you might find her surrounded by books and fairies toiling in her studio that never sleeps in South County, Missouri. You are welcome to follow her on many social platforms.

Once in a lifetime, if you're lucky, you meet someone who changes your life forever. They inspire you and teach you and without even trying. You crave their energy and their company like a drug – always looking on the bright

side, always creating something new, always making things happen. The time has come for the world to know her name and it will never be the same. — Y. Brazeal

Debbie delights everyone around her by taking ideas and turning them into reality. She begins projects with a creative spark, ignites them further with thoughtful purpose and planning, then meticulously fans the flames with her passion until she has produced a glowing fire. — A. Beckmann

Keep reading...I'm only going to get better. — D. Nuessle

Contact

nuessled@yahoo.com
facebook.com/nuessled
instagram.com/dustycharmdesigns
etsy.com/shop/dustycharmdesigns
facebook.com/dustycharmdesigns
hoodscoop03.com

Disclaimer

This fictional book is the result of a very active thought process. Names, characters, businesses, and places came about by slamming 50,000 words into a laptop, then editing like a wizard looking for the perfect spell. Any likeness to anything or anyone real is purely coincidental. Fairies, on the other hand (in my opinion) are very real and are everywhere. I've personally never met one, and was left no choice, than to creat them with my mind's magic. Typos you might find are simply the remnants of glitter that didn't quite stick to the page.

Made in the
USA
Monee, IL